No Teachers Left Behind

By HBF Teacher

Although many of the incidences that occur in this book may resemble real life events, this book is a work of fiction. The characters, incidents, and dialogue are drawn from the author's imagination and are not to be construed as real. Any semblance to actual events or persons, living or dead, is entirely coincidental.

FIRST EDITION

ISBN 10: 0-9747570-5-5

ISBN 13: 978-0-9747570-5-6

To the greatest teachers of all,

My mother and My grandmother.

And to all those who truly

Believe you're never too old to learn.

No Teachers Left Behind

The Leading Characters (Because a public school is more confusing than the United States Congress)

Administrators

1) Alicia Marsha - Principal/Vilyon Middle School, five years

2) Samuel Martin - Assistant Principal: Activities and Connections, 1st year

3) Carey Robinson – Assistant Principal: Textbooks and Technology, 1st year

4) April Simmons – Assistant Principal: Curriculum and Instruction, 1st year

5) Althea Johnson – Assistant Principal: Seventh grade, 2nd year

6) Malcolm Dowell – Assistant Principal: Sixth grade, 3rd year

7) Katie Pitts – Assistant Principal: Eighth grade, 1st year

8) Katy Holmes – Administrative Assistant to the Principal, 2nd year

Sixth Grade Teachers

9) Tammy Eigers – Teacher: Sixth Grade Language Arts, 1st year

10) Tracey Peterson – Teacher: Sixth Grade Language Arts, 2nd year

11) Peter Pilsher – Teacher: Sixth Grade Social Studies, 1st year

12) Amanda Schulman – Teacher: Sixth Grade Gifted/Math and Science, 9th year

13) Janice Thompson – Teacher: Sixth Grade Science, 3rd year

14) Anthony Vickers – Teacher: Sixth Grade Language Arts, 20th year

15) Marcus Watts – Teacher: Sixth Grade Science, 6th year

16) Shawna White – Teacher: Sixth Grade Math, 3rd year

17) Sandra Wyatt – Teacher: Sixth Grade Math, 4th year

Seventh Grade Teachers

18) Laverne Anderson – Teacher: Seventh Grade Science, 29th year

19) Sonya Harte – Teacher: Seventh Grade Social Studies, 8th year

20) Gail Jenkins – Teacher: Seventh Grade Science, 4th year

21) Sarah Parks – Teacher: Seventh Grade Language Arts, 1st year

22) Janet Wilson – Teacher: Seventh Grade Gifted/Math and Science, 8th year

Eighth Grade Teachers

23) Harold Jones – Teacher: Eighth Grade Social Studies, 5th year

24) Paul Jettison – Teacher: Eighth Grade Math, 3rd year

25) Louise Morgan – Teacher: Eighth Grade Math, 16th year

26) Jackson Myers – Teacher: Eighth Grade Language Arts, 1st year

27) Samantha Rogers – Teacher: Eighth Grade Gifted/Math and Science, 7th year

28) Sheila Valkrie – Teacher: Eighth Grade Math, 8th year

29) Angela Williams – Teacher: Eighth Grade Math, 6th year

Connections Teachers

30) Sharon Simmons – Teacher: Physical Education (all grades)

31) Coach Jeremy Lazarsky – Teacher: Physical Education (all grades)

Support Staff

32) Jack Lincoln – Superintendent of Schools

33) Margaret Bascombe – School Nurse

34) Leslie Longmire – Head Custodian

35) Gerald Smith – Supply Manager

36) Natalie Mitchell – Front Desk Receptionist

37) Patricia Hunte – Front Desk Receptionist

38) Christine Lawson – Front Desk/Clerical

39) Albert Lincoln – Technology Specialist

40) Paul Amin – Cafeteria Manager

41) Michael Henderson – Head Counselor

42) Alison Smith – Media Specialist

Students

43) Jamal – 8th grade student (2nd year)

44) Michael – 8th grade student (2nd year)

45) Jared – 6th grade student (generally AWOL)

46) Kelly Wyatt – 8th grade student (2nd year)

47) Sheneice Johnson – 8th grade student (2nd year)

Parents

48) Sally Walker – mother of Jeremy, 6th grade student

49) Maria Ramirez – mother of Hector, 6th grade student

***

Chipped paint, faulty wiring

and broken desks sit

in one tiny classroom.

Too many students.

Too few books.

Two job-carrying parents

of latch key kids who desire nothing

more than a free lunch.

They hate, without knowing,

the teachers who dare to care.

***

Morning Announcement:

"Good morning students. This is your principal Alicia Marsh. On behalf of all the staff members here at Vilyon Middle School, Home of the Valiant, let me welcome you to school today. This is a fantastic time for us to be here. It is a time for learning, a time for making new friends, a time for shaping futures for you and for future generations. As I walked among your bright, shining faces today, I felt blessed to be working here at such a wonderful school. Out of all the Middle schools in Taylor County, out of all the Middle Schools in the state of Georgia, out of all the Middle Schools in the United States and even the world, this is the very best school. I thank you in advance for being the best that you can be today. I thank you for going to your classes prepared and with your mind focused on learning. I thank you for being courteous to your peers, your teachers, and every person you come into contact with. All in all, I simply thank you for coming today and giving me an opportunity to live with you. As always, please know that you are cared about at Vilyon Middle School. If there is anything I can do to help you, please do not hesitate to drop by my office. Have a great day, students."

***

"She's joking right," Jamal said as he passed his friend Michael a Cola bottle laced with whiskey in the eighth grade restroom. The two of them rarely made it to homeroom for the morning announcements. "That white bitch is crazy. She don't know nothing about us, but pretends that she like us. She just needs to shut her damn mouth."

"I know what you mean man," said Michael before he took a long swig from the bottle. He swished the whiskey back and forth in his mouth before swallowing. "First, Moms make me come up here, and then I have to listen to that shit. I'm just here to get some booty and to hang out with you and my homeys. I don't even know if I'm gonna keep coming back. Once my old man gets out of his state-sponsored vacation, I'm out of here. I ain't getting nothing by coming here every day." He felt the whiskey burn his throat and travel its way to his stomach.

"Good thing too because I might have to hurt somebody. Mrs. Morgan is driving me up the wall talking about all the expectations she has for me. I got something for her all right."

"Well, you know what I say," Jamal said with a grin, "do unto others before they do unto you."

***

Michael tried to step around Mrs. Morgan, his forty-two year old math teacher. He was ready to go back inside the classroom and finish his morning nap.

"What's the point of coming to school if you're not going to bring paper, pencils, and your textbooks, Michael? What is this, your second year in eighth grade? Are you working on the five-year plan? Mrs. Morgan asked. She firmly placed her hands on her hip, as if scolding him with her stance. "Your test scores show that you are a capable young man, but you are not applying yourself. I believe in you. When are you going to believe in yourself? Her beady eyes squinted as she waited for an answer.

"I don't know why you brought me out here in the hall in the first place," he yelled. "I wasn't doing anything to anyone. I was minding my own damn business."

"Of course you weren't bothering anyone," Mrs. Morgan spoke in an even tone as she sidestepped out of

Michael's way. "How can you bother anyone when you are sleeping? Are you not getting enough sleep at home Michael?"

"Don't get in my face lady. I'm going to sit back down," Michael responded in a hostile tone. Morgan was really getting on his nerves. Her thick glasses looked so stupid on her stupid face. One more word and he'd rip that blade out of his pocket, and this was going to be her last living day on the planet.

Mrs. Morgan sighed loudly. "That's your choice then. Please make sure it's the right one."

"You're right, it is my choice," Michael said as he stepped around her and went back into the classroom, slamming the door behind him.

***

From: Alicia Marsh/Vilyon Middle School/TCPS

To: All Certified Staff

Re: Students to my office

Dear Friends,

Please ignore my last statement on this morning's announcements, and please do not give your students passes to come to my office. As much as I would like to spend time with each and every one of them, unfortunately, I am quite busy managing the school. Please collect written statements from the students who wish to see me. If any of the requests are urgent and require adult assistance, please deal with it accordingly by using your best logic.

As always, I thank you for following instructions and for allowing me to do my job of supporting you and our students.

Thanks for all you do,

Alicia Marsh

Principal, Vilyon Middle School

***

Teachers should never ask

for more than they have.

Asking is the same as complaining,

and then it becomes the teacher's fault.

***

Seventh grade teachers - forty of them crammed into the school's too-small conference room - sat impatiently around the finger-smudged wooden table and waited for Mrs. Johnson, their Assistant Principal, to speak. It was before school hours, but this came along with the job.

"As your grade level administrator, it is my duty to help you," Mrs. Johnson said. Her fire-red hair glowed under the florescent lighting. "Please let me know how I can help. If you need something, don't be shy; raise your hands."

There was some shuffling of feet and crossing and uncrossing of legs as the group of teachers looked around the room to see if anyone would be brave enough to ask for anything. Raising one's hand meant that enough had not been done, and if that was the case, rather than admit it, Mrs. Johnson would search for something that needed to be done - specifically by the person who had the nerve to suggest her grade level was not being run as well as it should be.

Slowly, Mrs. Anderson, the elderly science teacher, raised her hand. "My pencil sharpener does not work," she said in a low voice.

"Thank you," said Mrs. Johnson. "That is a problem. Now let's see you find a solution."

Mrs. Anderson's face grew red as she looked around the room at her peers. Most of them were looking down at the floor. She fiddled with her blue polyester collar. "Well the solution would be to have a custodian fix it."

"Hmmm...." Mrs. Johnson responded thoughtfully. A small smirk played at the corner of her lips. "A solution is something *you* do, not work that you make for others to do. Let me see. Oh, I have it. Why don't you buy an electric sharpener? Good ones last several years, and no one has to be bothered. Isn't that a great idea?"

"Well I ..." Mrs. Anderson tried to answer, but she was quickly interrupted by Mrs. Johnson.

"Mrs. Anderson, by any chance, have you turned in those address verification forms to me yet?"

"No, not yet. I have been—"

Mrs. Johnson cut her off. "Then let's work on that problem first, alright? Does anyone else need help with anything?"

***

Janice Thompson stormed into her co-worker's classroom. "I'm so pissed," she said, hastily plopping on a desk.

Anthony Vickers stared at her. "What is it now?" he asked in a resigned voice. He had been teaching Language Arts for twenty years. Nothing surprised him now because he had seen it all.

"Jared Mughinson."

"How can you be pissed at him?" Anthony asked. "He's usually at school, but rarely in class. He's like the perfect student."

"That is part of the problem," Janice said. She flicked her brown curly hair away from her eyes. Her face looked tired. "I followed procedure which was to let Mary Hunter know when someone has excessive absences. Do you know what she said?"

"She told you to call his home, right?"

Janice shook her head affirmatively, and then some uncontrollable force overtook her. She couldn't help it; she began to sob. "What do we have clerical people and counselors for? And when I spoke to the counselor, she also took the time to mention that I had not turned in those surveys she wanted. How am I supposed to turn in all the paperwork, play truant officer, and teach at the same time?" She gulped breaths of air, and tried to control herself. She wondered what Anthony thought of her sobbing like this. She wiped under her eyes.

Anthony reached over and patted her on the shoulder. "You do what you can in one day. That's all I can say. Your first priority is to teach the kids. Always remember that. Everything else either gets done or it doesn't despite what everybody tells you."

"Well I think that is easier said than done," Janice replied solemnly.

***

From: Alicia Marsh/Vilyon Middle School/TCPS

To: All Certified Staff

Re: Attendance

Dear Friends,

I know you are busy nurturing young minds, and I am quite sure you have better things to do than read e-mails during the day, but this e-mail is of an urgent nature. Please remember to take your attendance each class. This is important, not only for safety reasons, but also because our yearly budget is based on attendance.

Thanks for all you do,

Alicia Marsh

Principal, Vilyon Middle School

***

"Did you hear about Mr. Jackson?" Sharon, the PE teacher asked as she reached for her morning coffee.

Her teaching partner, Coach Lazarsky, replied, "No, what about him?"

"He's gone."

"What do you mean gone?"

"One of the students accused him of sexually harassing her."

"Shaun Jackson, our Shaun Jackson, sixty-one-year-old Shaun Jackson with the bad hip, National Teacher of the Year Shaun Jackson with over twenty five years of experience, a wife, six kids and eight grandchildren, one of them who goes to our school?"

"Yep," Sharon said sadly, "the very same one."

"Who would make up a story like that about him?"

"Kelly Wyatt. You remember her, don't you?"

Coach Lazarsky frowned. He pinched the bridge of

his nose with his fingers. "Yeah, I remember her. She was in one of our gym classes last year. She tried to wear those Daisy Dukes to class instead of the regulation shorts. Yeah, I remember her. Didn't she get kicked out last year for having sex in the janitor's closet with her boyfriend? Isn't she the one with a kid too?"

"That's the one I am talking about."

"Well, are they really taking her seriously? I cannot believe anybody would listen to a word she has to say. She was kicked out of school for a year for trying to cheat on that national test, remember?"

"Well, you know they have to investigate. It's the law," Sharon replied.

"Man that's awful. Shaun is such a good person. I hope he doesn't let the pressure get to him. I'll go talk to him when I get a break."

"Too late for that," Sharon said. "They said he was so pissed, he just packed up his stuff and walked right out the door after they told him they would have to look into

it." She sipped her coffee - needed to add more sugar. It

tasted too bitter.

***

What do teachers need?

Not desk or chairs

even though they come in handy.

Not copy paper and textbooks

although they make learning easier.

It is not computers and projectors

even though they make lessons more exciting.

What do teachers need?

They need support.

***

Her feet aching, Gail Jenkins walked around her class as her students took their Science pretests. She wanted to sit and rest her callused feet, but she didn't want Mrs. Marsh, the school's principal, to catch her sitting down again.

"Teachers should never sit down," according to Marsh. "Your students are unattended if you're sitting down."

Suddenly, Leslie, the head custodian, poked her head inside the classroom door. "Can I see you for a moment Mrs. Jenkins?" she asked.

What the hell was she bitching about now? Gail asked herself. That woman was crazy. Everybody knew that Leslie and her entire staff spent more time complaining about cleaning than they actually did working. Gail took one last glance around the classroom and met Leslie in the hallway.

"Have you sent any girls to the restroom lately?" Leslie asked with her hands on her hips. The woman couldn't be older than forty, but the wrinkles etched in her face suggested otherwise.

"A few. Why?"

"There's a maxi-pad stuck on the bathroom wall," Leslie responded. "I want to know who did it."

"Did you take it off the wall?" Mrs. Jenkins asked in a hushed tone.

"No," Leslie replied in a monotone voice. "I want to know who did it."

Mrs. Jenkins rolled her eyes and tried to bite her tongue, but she couldn't. "My God, you are a Rhodes scholar, aren't you? There are over 300 girls on this floor, and you come knocking on my damn door. Go take the damn pad down you fucking rocket scientist."

And with that, Mrs. Jenkins, forty-year teaching veteran, went back to her class wondering if Leslie would go door-to-door on the seventh grade hallway in search of

the maxi-pad culprit. It wouldn't surprise her.

***

From: Alicia Marsh/Vilyon Middle School/TCPS

To: All Certified Staff

Re: Meals

Dear Colleagues,

Unfortunately due to the number of fights we have had today (and yes we have had quite a few), we will be having the rest of today's meals in the classrooms. Teachers, I know this will take away from your scheduled rest breaks, but it is imperative that we place the needs of our students before our own needs. Hopefully, this situation will be cleared up tomorrow, and we can go back to our regular cafeteria schedule.

Thanks for putting our kids first,

Alicia Marsh

Principal, Vilyon Middle School

P.S – I will be off campus today during lunch. My husband is taking me to the Olive Garden.

***

From: Gail Jenkins/Vilyon Middle School/TCPS

To: Sarah Parks

Re: Do you think they read our e-mails?

Do you think they read our e-mails? I really hope they do.

Mrs. Marsh needs to know that she is a straight out bitch!

Gail Jenkins

7th grade Science, Vilyon Middle School

***

From: Sarah Parks/Vilyon Middle School/TCPS

To: Gail Jenkins

Re: Do you think they read our e-mails?

If they did read our e-mails, both of us would be unemployed. Heard you cussed out Leslie today. Is it true? If so, I hope you gave her enough hell for everybody. I don't even know her that well, but it seems like she has been running things around here for way too long. When did custodians become more important than everyone else in the school building?

Sarah Parks

7th grade Language Arts, Vilyon Middle School

***

From: Gerald Smith/Vilyon Middle School/TCPS

To: All Certified and Clerical Staff

Re: Paper Supplies

Due to the budget crisis, you will not be receiving your copy paper or printer ink allotment at this time. I know how resourceful you all are, so I am sure that you will have no problems finding alternative means of distributing information. If I can be of further assistance, please do not hesitate to fill out a request form located on the door of my office.

As always, thanks for your understanding and patience. It's a great time to go green. Remember to recycle.

Gerald Smith

Supply Manager, Vilyon Middle School

***

"Everybody is saying that he's gay."

"Who are we talking about?" Natalie, the front desk receptionist said as she walked into the office from her fifth coffee break of the day. Her tight pencil skirt was a bit questionable—some students were getting reprimanded for wearing skirts too short—but Natalie would defend her attire. "I sit behind a desk all day," she'd say.

Her co-workers, Christine and Patricia, smiled.

"You know who," Patricia giggled. "Mr. Pilsher." She twirled her hair with her fingers.

"He is not gay," Natalie said. She pulled out a compact make-up mirror and checked to see if her lipstick was smeared.

"Oh please," said Christine, "that man is waaaaay too pretty to be straight, and he is so nice."

"I don't think you guys should be so quick to judge him," responded Natalie.

Christine and Patricia glanced at each other.

"He is nice enough," said Patricia. "At least he ain't bitchy like the rest of the teachers around here. We need more like him and less like the rest of them. Too many of these teachers walk around like their shit don't stink."

"Ugh, seriously," Natalie said grooming her eyebrows. "If it wasn't for us at the front desk, this place would be falling down."

***

From: Alicia Marsh/Vilyon Middle School/TCPS

To: Gail Jenkins

Re: Personnel conflict

Dear Ms. Jenkins,

Recently I was made aware of an altercation that occurred

between you and our head custodian. I am not sure of the

exact circumstance, but I can only assume that you were

having a stressful day and allowed your personal problems

to interfere with your work.   If you need time off, please

let your grade level administrator know.   Be aware that any

days taken off will be deducted from your sick bank.

Additionally, any non-emergency days taken off without

five days advance notice will be noted on your permanent

employment record.

Please remember that at Vilyon Middle School we are

family.   Everyone is loved here. Remember to show that

each day, not only to your students, but also to the people with whom you work.

Alicia Marsh

Principal, Vilyon Middle School

***

From: Albert Lincoln/Vilyon Middle School/TCPS

To: All Certified Staff

Re: Student Computer Set Up

I will be coming around to set up student computers in class as quickly as possible. I will visit the gifted classrooms first and then work my way through the rest of your classes. Thank you in advance for your patience.

Albert Lincoln

Technology Support Specialist, Vilyon Middle School

***

And of course, administrators don't show favoritism.

They're completely impartial

and they never forget

what you did not do for them or

how well your kids scored on the big test.

Better scores naturally mean better teaching, right?

The natural IQ of your students does not matter

or their willingness to learn.

Higher scores mean job security and a window with a view.

***

From: Paul Amin/Vilyon Middle School/TCPS

To: Certified Staff

Re: Breakfast items – please read!

Due to county regulations, all unused breakfast items must be returned to the cafeteria for auditing purposes. It is county policy that we throw away any unused breakfast items, so please return them to me or one of my staff members ASAP. I understand that some of your students may be hungry in the afternoons and would like to eat the leftovers, but county policy is county policy. Please remember to return the leftover items so that our paperwork will be in order.

Thanks for your help in keeping county policy,

Paul Amin

Cafeteria Manager, Vilyon Middle School

Mrs. Thompson walked slowly into the front office. Her legs ached from seventy years of life experience, but she held her head upright even though she used a cane to aid her every step. She carried a blue gift bag in one hand.

"Good morning," she said politely to the women in the front office who sat at the long desk in front of the window. Even though there were two of them, neither of the women responded to the greeting. Mrs. Thompson was quick to take note of both their names from their name badges. Christine was the red haired one wearing the low cut tight sweater, and Patricia was the one with the blonde bob who popped her gum incessantly.

Just as Mrs. Thompson was about to speak, the phone rang, and she waited for one of them to answer it.

"It's your turn," Patricia said in between pops as she reached into a nearby drawer and removed a nail file.

Christine rolled her eyes. "I answered the last

one."

The phone continued to ring. Mrs. Thompson
looked from one staff member to the other

"No, you didn't girl." Patricia pointed the nail file
at Christine. "I did cause that lady was calling about a free
lunch, and I told her to come and get a form from the
cafeteria."

"I assume that at least one of you is actually paid to
answer the phone here," Mrs. Thompson remarked in a
voice loud enough to be heard over the phone.

Christine and Patricia shot her hostile glares.

Mrs. Thompson met them with her own icy stare.
She wasn't used to be ignored, not at her age.

Christine sighed loudly and reluctantly reached for
the phone. "Thanks for calling Vilyon Middle School.
I'm having a great day and I hope you are too." Her beauty
pageant words did not match her cold smile.

"And what can I do for you?" Patricia asked Mrs.

Thompson in a haughty voice.

Mrs. Thompson cleared her throat and said, "I would like to see Mr. Jettison.   I have something for him."

Patricia took her gum out of mouth. "What you got?"

Mrs. Thompson could not believe the attitude. How times have changed. "What business is it of yours? Mr. Jettison's is my grandson's teacher, and I have the right to see him.   Mrs. Marsh and I are old friends too. She told me I was welcome to visit whenever I can. She and I go to the same church too. Why don't…"

Christine placed the phone on its receiver and gave Patricia a warning look.

"Unfortunately, Mr. Jettison is in class right now. We're sorry that you came at a bad time.   Would you like to leave a message?"

Mrs. Thompson glanced at her watch. "It's only 9:40."

"Classes start at 9:30," Patricia said in a matter of fact voice before she shoved another piece of gum in her mouth.

"Oh, I thought they started later." Mrs. Thompson looked down at the blue bag.

"We can give that to him for you," offered Christine.

"I'd rather give him the brownies myself. He had my grandson Kevin last year, and he taught him so well. Now, he has Marvin this year. Mr. Jettison is a great teacher. He teaches, and he cares. He loves my brownies too, that's why I want to make sure he gets them. I don't want someone else eating them or having my brownies sit around for a week. I baked them fresh this morning."

Patricia extended her hand out towards Mrs. Thompson. "You don't have to worry about them just sitting around. We'll make sure they get to the right person."

Mrs. Thompson looked down at the bag again.
"I'm not sure. Maybe I'll sit here and wait for his break.
He does get a break, doesn't he?"

The phone rang again. Christine stared at Patricia.
Patricia waited a second before she reluctantly picked up
the phone. "Thanks for calling Vilyon Middle School. I'm
having a great day, and I hope you are too."

"He gets a planning period, but I don't think it's
until the end of the day," replied Christine. "That's a long
time away, maybe 3:00pm."

Mrs. Thompson exhaled loudly. She was already
exhausted simply from dealing with these two. She figured
it would probably be easier to drop off a package at the
White House. "Oh okay," she agreed. "Just make sure he
gets it today and preferably soon." She handed the bag
over to Christine. "Give him a message for me too please."

"Sure thing." Christine smiled brightly.

"Hold on a minute," Patricia told her caller as she

put the phone on hold and placed the receiver down. Her curiosity was killing her.

"Tell him that Cathy Thompson says we don't have enough good teachers," said Mrs. Thompson. "Tell him that he's appreciated everyday, at least by me."

Christine held the bag in both hands as though it was a priceless item. "We will. Thank you so much for coming out today."

"No, thank you." Mrs. Thompson smiled for the first time since she entered the office. "Your kindness is appreciated too."

"You said your name was Cathy Thompson, right?" Patricia asked as she looked up from a notepad where she was presumably writing Mrs. Thompson's message.

"That's correct."

Christine nodded. "Just want to make sure we deliver the correct message."

"Well thank you again," Mrs. Thompson said before turning around and walking out of the office.

Patricia watched the hold light disappear on the phone as the caller finally hung up. Then she glanced at Christine who was watching Mrs. Thompson walk towards her car.

"Old bitch." Christine reached into the bag and pulled out a white box with a blue ribbon tied around its center and passed it to her friend.

Patricia stuck her gum under the bottom side of the drawer and then quickly cut the ribbon. "I don't care if she knows the Pope. Who the hell does she think she is?" She opened the box and held it out for Christine.

Without a second's thought, Christine grabbed one of the white chocolate brownies and bit into it. "Mmmm....," she moaned. "That old heifer can really bake."

Patricia followed her lead and bit into a brownie. She moaned and then took another huge bite. The phone rang as they polished off the entire box.

When she and Christine finished patting their bellies, Patricia looked up Mrs. Thompson's address on the computer and wrote a thank you note from Mr. Jettison. She wanted to make sure she and Christine would have more brownies to enjoy.

***

From: Maria Ramirez@yahoo.com

To: Janice Thompson

Re: H. Ramirez

Dear Ms. Thompson,

I am Hector's mother. I am writing to let you know that

Hector cannot do homework on Tuesdays, Thursdays, and

on the weekends due to his football practice and game

schedule. Please do not give him a zero on these days. If

you have any questions, please do not hesitate to e-mail me

or call.

Sincerely Yours,

Maria Ramirez

***

From: Janice Thompson/Vilyon Middle School/TCPS

To: Maria Ramirez

Re: H. Ramirez

Dear Mrs. Ramirez,

I am happy that Hector has outside interests, but Hector has to do his homework in order for him to be successful and pass my class. If Hector does not complete all of his homework, it will be hard for him to pass my tests and earn the required passing grades in all of his classes. This is Hector's second year in the sixth grade, and we would like to see him graduate to the seventh grade next year. Please do not hesitate to write or e-mail me if you have additional concerns.

Thanks for your continued support,

Janice Thompson,

6th grade Science, Vilyon Middle School

***

From: Maria Ramirez@yahoo.com

To: Janice Thompson

Re: H. Ramirez

Dear Ms. Thompson, I do not think you like Mexicans very much; I think you are racist. If you give Hector a bad grade, I am going to call the Superintendent of Schools and tell him that you do not like Mexicans.   Hector had better not have a bad grade in your class or else.

Sincerely Yours,
Maria Ramirez

***

From: Michael Henderson/Vilyon Middle School/TCPS

To: Alicia Marsh

Re: Counselor for Teachers

Dear Mrs. Marsh,

I am writing to follow-up regarding our recent conversation about providing a counselor for the staff members. I do believe that it will increase morale and help the staff members, especially the teachers who deal with a huge amount of stress in their lives. If you recall, we had two staff members who had heart attacks earlier this year. Of course, we cannot assume that this was entirely related to work, but we both know that any type of job is an additional stress. If we cannot afford to hire an additional counselor, I and Mrs. Vaughn, the sixth grade counselor, will be willing to meet with staff members as needed when we are not meeting with students. Once again, I believe this would be an invaluable resource for our staff.

I look forward to hearing from you soon.

Be Well,

Michael Henderson

Chief Counselor, Vilyon Middle School

***

What is an administrator's job?

Is it to meet the whims of the students?

To give in to the parents?

Comply with the demands of the district office?

Or meet the needs of the staff?

Or to don a cape and fly about the school screaming:

"I am the Boss!

Laugh at my bad jokes and

kiss my ass or else!"

***

From: Alicia Marsh/Vilyon Middle School/TCPS

To: Michael Henderson

Re: Staff Counselor

Dear Michael,

Thank you for your e-mail regarding the counselor issue. Unfortunately, I am unable to allow you to provide this service for our staff members. It is your job to care for our students, not our staff members. Any staff member who needs counseling should seek treatment outside of the school grounds. I trust you to remember the reason why you were hired and focus all of your energy and ideas on the care of our students. If any staff member (and please share this information with your counseling staff) comes to you for personal assistance, he/she should be directed to the health care provider notebook that was given to them at orientation. Additionally, please also send me the names of any staff members who seek assistance. I want to make sure that they are mentally capable of managing a

classroom on a daily basis.

Thanks again for your e-mail,

Alicia Marsh

Principal, Vilyon Middle School

***

From: Malcolm Dowell/Vilyon Middle School/TCPS

To: Maria Ramirez

CC: Marcus Watts

BCC: Janice Thompson

Re: Student Reassignment

Dear Mrs. Ramirez,

I'm sorry to hear that you are unhappy with Hector's schedule. My apologies that Hector was placed in the same teacher's classroom again. I understand that you would like for your child to learn under different teachers each year. With that in mind, I have changed Hector's schedule so he will have a new Science teacher, Mr. Watts. Mr. Watts is a veteran teacher with several years of experience. He is passionate about his teaching, and he works very hard to make sure his students enjoy learning. If I can be of further assistance, please do not hesitate to e-mail me or call. I'm always available to help you.

Best Wishes,

Malcolm Dowell

6th grade Assistant Principal, Vilyon Middle School

***

From: Alicia Marsh/Vilyon Middle School/TCPS

To: All Certified Staff

Re: Attendance (2nd request)

Dear Staff Members,

It is imperative that you take attendance for each class that you have. Once again, this is important, not only for safety reasons but also because our budget is based on attendance. A list of those teachers who are not taking attendance will be documented. If you have any questions regarding this policy, please do not hesitate to contact one of the assistant principals immediately. I will be in and out of my office throughout the day.

Alicia Marsh

Principal, Vilyon Middle School

***

"I thought you were leaving Sharon," Coach Lazarsky said when he saw her reentering the gym.

Sharon grimaced. "I am still nauseous, but it is just way too much work to find a sub." She ran her fingers through her sweaty hair.

"Nobody in the front office can help you?" he asked.

"Christine was quick to remind me that the front office staff must be notified twenty-four hours in advance in order to find a sub. School policy."

"School policy my ass," the Coach replied. "She is a lazy bitch."

***

Ms. Pitts, a tall blonde wearing a dark blue skirt suit that stopped just above her knees, called to the man who had just left the mailroom. "Mr. Myers, hold on."

The athletic man who resembled Matt Damon turned around reluctantly. "Hello Ms. Pitts," he responded. "Can I help you with something?" This was his first teaching position since he had finished college, so he was very nervous that his grade level principal had stopped him. He had seriously hoped that with all the teachers at the two thousand-student school, she wouldn't have had time to learn his name.

"No, no," Katie said quickly. A huge smile lit up her face. "I just wanted to know if I could help you with anything. I know this is your first year here, and it's also mine as an administrator. I still remember my first teaching position. I was very stressed out the first year."

Jackson Myers breathed a huge sigh of relief. He had heard horror stories about some administrators. "I think I'm doing all right," he said after a moment's reflection. "I've always believed in treating others how I want to be treated, so most of the kids are treating me okay, I guess."

Katie's smile grew wider. "I'm happy. I want all my teachers to say that. But if it wasn't true, you would tell me, wouldn't you?"

"Yeah, I would tell you," he admitted out loud and to himself. There was something about her that seemed sincere. It was like she really cared, and he found that very refreshing.

***

From: Marcus Watts/Vilyon Middle School/TCPS

To: Janice Thompson

Re: H. Ramirez

My God Janice, what have you done this time? Why do I have to get your hand-me-downs? You know I'm trying to get students out of my class, not in. Who have you pissed off now? Why can't there be just one year where you don't get into trouble?

Marcus Watts

6th grade Science, Vilyon Middle School

P.S – Are you still coming to my house party on Saturday?

***

"What's up Kel Kel?" Sheneice asked her friend. She turned around in her desk, ignoring Mr. Myers as he lectured on something completely boring. Language Arts class was so fucking pointless. "It is true what I heard girl?" she whispered.

Kelly leaned forward and spoke softly. "What did you hear?" she asked as she tried to hide a growing smile.

"You got rid of Jackson."

"Damn right I did," Kelly said. She unraveled a purple jolly rancher and popped it in her mouth. "I told that old bastard not to fail me, and he did. I even offered to let him touch my titties, but the old fart wanted to be so self-righteous. Threatened to call my parents. I couldn't let that happen." She slid the candy in and out of her mouth seductively.

"Jose saw him leaving and said the old man was crying and shit," Sheneice laughed.

"Well, that's what he get," Kelly said. She sat up straight, stuck her chest out, and eyed Mr. Myers. He was young, and he was fine. She hated Language Arts, but she was going to get an A this year. There was no doubt about it. Myers would play or pay; it was that simple.

***

From: Janice Thompson/Vilyon Middle School/TCPS

To: Marcus Watts

Re: H. Ramirez

Whatever loser!   I hope you enjoy Hector because if he gives you any shit, which he will, then his mother is going to be all over your ass, accusing you of racism and whatever crap she can think of.   He's dumb as dirt. Mix that in with lazy as hell, and the boy should drop out now and learn the phrase, "Would you like fries or onion rings with that." Or maybe he shouldn't even worry about learning that because if too many people learn it, then his mother might not have a job anymore.   Ignorant ass family! More power to you.

Janice Thompson

6th grade Science, Vilyon Middle School

***

From: Samuel Martin/Vilyon Middle School/TCPS

To: 930 Certified Staff

Re: Activity Nominations

As we continue this school year, it is important to remember the significance of nurturing the whole child. Here at Vilyon Middle School, we take great pride in being able to offer our students a wide range of activities. Still, it is imperative that we make sure each student is correctly matched with an activity that will best suit him or her. As you fill in recommendation forms for your students, please keep the following in mind:

1) No student who is not in a gifted/honors class should be encouraged to join Reader's Rally, The Science or Math Club, the Debate Team, or the Academic Bowl Squad.

2) No student who received more than 3 referrals in the past school year is eligible for participating in

extracurricular activities unless their parents are active members of the PTSA.

3) All students who participate in extracurricular activities must have a 3.0 or higher GPA.

4) Exceptions will be made for members of our Boys basketball team who took state last year. Go Valiants!

If you have additional questions, please forward them to Christine Lawson, our school clerk. She will forward them to me.

Thanks so much for your attention to this e-mail,

Samuel Martin

Assistant Principal - Activities and Connections, Vilyon Middle School

***

From: Marcus Watts/Vilyon Middle School/TCPS

To: Janice Thompson

Re: H. Ramirez

One of you needs to sign up for an anger management class

or something.   What's going on with you, girl?   Who

pissed in your cornflakes this morning?

Marcus Watts

6th grade Science, Vilyon Middle School

***

From: Gerald Smith/Vilyon Middle School/TCPS

To: All Certified and Clerical Staff

Re: Paper Supplies

Staff,

Paper supplies have arrived. Each teacher will receive one pack of copy paper and one ink cartridge. Please note that this should last you the entire school year. If for one reason or another, you run out of ink, extra cartridges are available for sale at cost. If needed, this purchase can also be directly debited in equal installments from your paycheck.

Happy Printing,

Gerald Smith

Supply Manager, Vilyon Middle School

***

From: Janice Thompson/Vilyon Middle School/TCPS

To: Marcus Watts

Re: H. Ramirez

I'm so sick of this bullshit. When we ask for support from the administrators, we can't get anything, but if some illiterate parent calls the school and complains about us, then it's suddenly a situation that needs attention. The only time I ever heard from Hector's mother is when she saw her son's report card at the end of the year. You know we sent out report cards three times before that. She did not care at all until she discovered her son was not going to be promoted. That bitch did not show up for one parent conference last year or for the student support meeting. She never returned my phone calls or progress reports. She also completely ignored my tutoring offers. I offered to come in early in the morning and to stay late in the afternoons. I even said I would come in on Saturday mornings. I gave that boy extra credit which he never returned. I accepted work that was one and two months late. I did everything but take the tests for him. And now, Dowell is willing to hang me out to dry as a bad teacher rather than tell this lady that she and her son are both nothing but burdens on this country. You saw that e-mail, didn't you? The administrators don't give a damn about us and most of the parents don't either. It just really pissed me off, and I'm sick of it.

I will definitely be at your house party on Saturday. A party is just what I need. What is today? Monday. I might start drinking this afternoon. Let the pre-party begin.

Janice Thompson
6th grade Science, Vilyon Middle School

***

There is something about walking into your own classroom

After a long summer

when you honestly admit to actually missing your students.

Your classroom is like your second home.

As you unpack the boxes and dust off the furniture,

you realize just how much you love this place.

It's truly where you belong, where you feel alive

during those awesome, life-touching moments

where you actually teach something and see those eyes
light up with new knowledge.

Then the bell rings,

and they come in

with heavy chips on their shoulders

and their unwarranted hate.

Then you wonder again,

if you're not wasting your life.

***

From: Katie Pitts/Vilyon Middle School/TCPS

To: Alicia Marsh

Re: Metal Detectors

Dear Alicia,

Have you had time to rethink your position on metal detectors? I can understand your decision to not want them because you feel that their presence will imply that the school is unsafe to parents and the community. But, I do believe (and I have the statistics to prove it), the presence of the metal detectors actually promotes safety. Not only does it prevent students from bringing weapons, but it also makes the students feel safer. According to a National School Safety survey conducted last year, US students cited safety as their number one concern.

Please let me know when you are willing to discuss this important issue further. I am willing to come early or stay late to discuss it.

Thanks so much,

Katie Pitts, Assistant Principal – 8th Grade, Vilyon Middle School

***

From: Albert Lincoln/Vilyon Middle School/TCPS

To: All Certified Staff

Re: Printer Issues

In addition to setting up student computers, I am now working on the installation for Mrs. Marsh's new top-of-the-line computer system. At the same time, I am aware that many of you are having printer issues. Please be assured that as teachers, you are my top priority. For the next two days, I will be at a technology seminar in New York, but after that, I will be with each and every one of you as soon as possible, so please be patient and do not leave notes taped to my office door or send me e-mails.

Again, thank you for your patience,

Albert Lincoln

Technology Support Specialist, Vilyon Middle School

***

Laverne Anderson brushed a long gray strand out of her eyes and sat down in the lone chair in the mailroom. Her hands were filled with the magazines, newsletters, and school memos that seemed to collect in her mailbox by the seconds. There were so many things in those magazines that she wouldn't mind purchasing for her students to use, but most of them came with a hefty price tag. She certainly couldn't afford them. Even after twenty-nine years of teaching, she still barely made enough on which to live. Unfortunately, she had long ago maxed out her pay increases for tenure, and she knew she was way too old to go back to school to get her Master's Degree.

Nevertheless, she enjoyed her work. She liked watching her students discover their own knowledge in her class. More than that, she loved when they asked questions and then sought out their own answers. That alone made up for everything else she never received

***

From: Margaret Bascombe/Vilyon Middle School/TCPS

To: All Faculty and Staff

Re: CPR Training

Dear Teammates,

It is CPR training time again.   Now we can prepare

ourselves for life's unplanned emergencies.   If you have

not been certified and wish to be, please send me an e-mail

no later than Wednesday.   I cannot tell you how important

it is to have your CPR certification.   Just last week, a high

school student went to the movies with some friends.

When he had his heart attack, no one in the movie theater

was certified in CPR.   This child, a former student of ours,

died on the theater floor.   Doctors at the hospital later

stated that CPR could have saved this young man's life.

CPR is important.   It can make the difference between life

and death.   If you feel you are too busy to come in early or stay late for this invaluable class, do not think about

yourself, think about your students and your co-workers.

Hope to see you at the training,

Margaret Bascombe

School Nurse, Vilyon Middle School

***

"Okay everyone, thanks for coming to the Math curriculum meeting," said Mrs. Valkrie, the 8th grade Math contact leader, in her usual cold voice. "This is the meeting to plan the rest of the meetings for the school year. Tuesdays and Thursdays are best for me, so those will be our meeting days."

Mrs. Smith, a first year teacher, could not believe what she was hearing. As always, she found it hard to restrain herself from speaking. "Are we doing anything at this meeting besides planning additional meetings?"

Mrs. Valkrie looked at her haughtily. Her brown hair was pulled back in a bun so tight it stretched the skin on her face. "No, that's all that is on the agenda for this meeting."

"Geez," responded Mrs. Smith. "We had that early morning faculty meeting today, and then as soon as I got in my classroom, there was a meeting with my teammates.

Now this meeting, and then another one after this, and then there is one before we leave today.   When am I actually going to have a meeting where I make plans to teach?"

Paul Jettison, a third year teacher, laughed.   "You do that at home."

"My hours are from 8:30 to 4:30," insisted Mrs. Williams.   "When I'm at home, I plan on spending that time with my family."

"Such negativity," Mrs. Valkrie spoke and sent a line of saliva across the room. "This is not good at all for Vilyon.   We work here Mrs. Williams; we do not spend our time complaining. Every minute you spend complaining is another minute you can spend educating a child. If this is too stressful for you, then you might want to rethink your career. We care about our students at Vilyon and make sure our school meets its yearly goals."

***

From: Sonya Harte/Vilyon Middle School/TCPS

To: Angela Williams

Re: CPR Course

Two questions: Do we get more money if we obtain our CPR certifications? If we are certified, can we be prosecuted and/or fired if we refuse to give CPR to a particular student or staff member?   I am certainly not going to save the life of someone I absolutely despise. In that regard, I would be punishing myself, and I already get more than enough hell. I am so not a sadist.

Have a good day girl,

Sonya Harte

7th grade Social Studies, Vilyon Middle School

***

From: Angela Williams/Vilyon Middle School/TCPS

To: Sonya Harte

Re: CPR Course

You are insane! I'm not sure, but those are definitely valid questions. E-mail both the nurse and Mrs. Marsh and let me know—LMAO. Have you seen the new sixth grade teacher, Mr. Pilsher? He is so George Cloooney sexy that I can barely stand it. He parked next to me today; he drives a new Beemer. Nobody is sure what he was doing before he came here. He doesn't say a lot about himself, but he's really friendly and has an awesome smile. Unfortunately, Christine says that he is gay. Let me know if you find out anything before I do.

Keep Smiling,

Angela Williams

8th grade Math, Vilyon Middle School

From: Peter Pilsher/Vilyon Middle School/TCPS

To: Catherine.Pilsher.myheart@yahoo.com

Re: Love you!

Hi honey! Hope all is well.   The day is going so-so. Even though I am swamped, I still find myself looking at your picture on my desk.   I cannot believe I am lucky enough to have you as my wife.   I cannot wait to get home and finish what we started this morning.

Love you more than I can say,

Peter Pilsher

6th grade, Social Studies

***

From: Amanda Schulman/Vilyon Middle School/TCPS

To: 6th grade teachers

CC: Alison Smith (Media Specialist)

Re: Laptops

Because laptops have been improperly returned to the media center in the past—and it is creating extra work for the media specialists—6th grade laptops will now be stored in my classroom. You will need to see me if you would like to use them. They will be available on any day that the sixth grade gifted students are not using them.

Amanda Schulman

6th grade Gifted/Math and Science, Vilyon Middle School

***

Let them tell you it's about what you know,

but who gets the classroom with the window

and who always gets the corner room

next to the cafeteria,

Who gets the new desks and chairs,

Who always has the worst hall duty -

It's all about who you know.

***

From: Alicia Marsh/Vilyon Middle School/TCPS

To: Certified Staff

Re: Attendance at Basketball games

Good day colleagues,

This e-mail is to remind you that your contract stipulates

that you must work at least two VMS basketball games this

year. I understand that there has been some confusion to

this policy, and this e-mail should serve as clarification and

a final address to this matter. Yes, I do understand there

are some schools that do not require their teachers to work

basketball games; these schools require the athletes'

parents to do so. That is not the policy at VMS. Once

again, you are required to volunteer for at least two school

basketball games this year. Go ahead and view the

basketball schedule on your website and place the dates on

your calendar. Please view your contract and employee

handbook for further details. When you read your

contract, you will also note you do not receive additional pay for these Saturday morning events. The smiles of your students when they see you there should be payment enough. I can't tell you how often students come up to me and say how much they appreciate the staff support at the games.

Thanks for sharing yourself with our kids,
Alicia Marsh
Principal, Vilyon Middle School

***

"You got it?" Michael asked. There was nobody else in the boy's bathroom. Pee covered the tiled floor and somebody had written 'Kelly gives free blowjobs' above the mirror in permanent black marker.

"Yeah, I got it," replied Jamal. "You got my stuff?"

Michael pulled a 9mm from his jeans and extended his hand. "$100.00 man."

Jamal reached into his front pocket, took out a wad of cash, and smacked it into Michael's palm. Michael handed him the gun and then counted the money as Jamal checked out the weapon.

"We're good man," Michael said after several seconds. "I threw in one clip for you, but you gotta get your own."

"Thanks," Jamal said as he practiced aiming the gun at one of the stall doors.

Michael watched him and smiled. "Whoever is

messing with you is definitely messing with the wrong

nigga man.   I hate to be in his or her shoes"

***

From: Sonya Harte/Vilyon Middle School/TCPS

To: Angela Williams

Re: Basketball Games

I say we get two masks and jump Marsh's ass in the
parking lot tonight. What about you? We can beat her in
the damn head with a basketball or something. Saturday
morning is my sleep-in day, and I'm not getting up even if
my house is on fire. The firemen can just carry my bed out
with me in it. Weekends are what teachers live for. I
always wondered why the school would not give us any
glue for our projects. Now I know why. That crazy bitch
is sniffing it all up.

Sonya Harte
7th grade Social Studies, Vilyon Middle School

***

From: Alicia Marsh/Vilyon Middle School/TCPS

To: Katie Pitts

Re: Metal detectors

Katie,

I have looked at your proposal regarding the metal detectors. At this time, I still do not think they are necessary. Last year, although there were quite a few unsubstantiated rumors, we only had two incidences where weapons were brought to school. Both of these situations were quietly handled with no one being harmed.

Thanks again for thinking about school safety, but I would appreciate it if you let this issue go and instead focus on preparing your eighth graders for their standardized tests. Last year, the eighth graders had the worse scores out of all grade levels. Let's not let this happen again.

Alicia Marsh

Principal, Vilyon Middle School

***

From: Angela Williams/Vilyon Middle School/TCPS

To: Sonya Harte

Re: E-mail Policy

Dear Ms. Harte,

Please be aware that Taylor County Schools provides you with e-mail solely so that you can use it for instructional purposes. All e-mails are subject to administrative scanning. Anyone who uses the school e-mail for illegal, pornographic, and/or unauthorized purposes will lose computer access. If you have additional questions, please see your grade level, area administrator, or refer to your employee handbook.

ROFL!

Drinks at Island Breeze after work?

Angela Williams

8th grade Math, Vilyon Middle School

**

From: Malcolm Dowell/Vilyon Middle School/TCPS

To: 6th grade Teachers

Re: Meeting after school

Dear Teachers,

We will have a brief but mandatory meeting after school

today to discuss some important issues.   Please be

prepared to stay.   Those of you with children, please make

arrangements with a sitter during your planning.   This

meeting should not take more than two and a half hours.

Thanks for your cooperation,

Malcolm Dowell

6th grade Assistant Principal, Vilyon Middle School

***

From: Leslie Longmire/Vilyon Middle School/TCPS

To: All Faculty and Staff

Re: Soap in student restrooms

Because the students are emptying the soap containers and then using the soap along with permanent markers to write on the restroom walls, we are temporarily removing soap from the student restrooms. Please provide hand sanitizer in your classrooms for students as needed.

Thanks for helping us keep Vilyon clean,

Leslie Longmire

Head Custodian Vilyon Middle School

***

From: Kelly Scott@oohay.com

To: Tracey Peterson

Re: Marvin's Grades

Dear Ms. Peterson,

I am writing because Marvin texted me earrrlier and told

me that he is in your Englesh class again. I do not want

Marvin in your class again this year. You felled him last

year, so I have no idea why he was placed in your class

again.   You were bitch last year, and I am sure you are still

a bitch this year. You are an inqualified lady who has a job

as an educater, and you are also a very unsimpathetic

person. I insist that Marvin be placed in the class of a more

quallified teacher who is simpathetic to the fact that he

sometimes takes a nap during the day because he likes to

stay up late watching televission. I expect this to be done

before the end of the day, and I would like to receive an

email when it ocurs.   If this is not done, I will come to

Vilion as soon as my shift at the *Waffle Shack* is over.

Sincerely Yours,

Kelly Scott, Marvins mother

***

From: Tracey Peterson/ Vilyon Middle School/TCPS

To: Kelly Scott@oohay.com

Re: Marvin's Grades (politically correct – school supported e-mail – sent)

Dear Ms. Scott,

I am sorry to hear you are disappointed with Marvin's schedule. Unfortunately, because I am only a teacher, I am not allowed to make any schedule changes. I will forward your e-mail to my grade level administrator who has the authority to make your requested changes. Hopefully this change will allow Marvin to be as successful as he can be.

Best Wishes,

Tracey Peterson

6th grade Language Arts, Vilyon Middle School

***

From: Tracey Peterson/ Vilyon Middle School/TCPS

To: Kelly Scott@oohay.com

CC: Shawna White

Re: Marvin's Grades (remix – not sent)

Dear Ms. Scott,

I do not give a damn that you are unhappy with Marvin's grades. How the hell do you think I feel? That shit-for-brains kid of yours repeated the fourth and fifth grade TWICE, and now he is repeating the sixth grade for the second year in my class. That fat turd brought down my class average on the CRCT. He could not even bubble in his own name right to get the minimum score. And you, a waitress who works at a place where a waffle and hot dog platter is considered a gourmet dish, have the nerve to criticize me without even recognizing the fact that this boy —who is almost old enough to drive himself to school — does not even know his multiplication tables. How many certifications do you need in order to be a waitress and a sad-ass parent? I had to be certified in order to get my job. You are a dumb bitch. If Marvin is the future of this world, where in the hell is the damn red button? Fuck you bitch and the entire family that inbred you.

Please send additional comments to my personal e-mail account: uignorantbitch@feelme.com.

Tracey Peterson

6th grade Language Arts, Vilyon Middle School

***

From: Shawna White/Vilyon Middle School/TCPS

To: Tracey Peterson

Re: Marvin's Grades

Girl, please tell me that you did not send that e-mail out!   I cannot afford to feed both of us. Thanks for helping us increase parent support ☺

Shawna White

6th grade Math, Vilyon Middle School

P.S.—Do you think I should invite Mr. Pilsher out for drinks?

***

From: Tracey Peterson/ Vilyon Middle School/TCPS

To: Shawna White

Re: E-mail

Shawna, if you really think I sent that e-mail out, then you and Mrs. Scott must both share the same crack pipe. As for Mr. Pilsher, he is definitely hot, but I heard he was gay. Hey, but let me know if he is not gay. I might have to give you a run for your money.

Tracey Peterson

6th grade Language Arts, Vilyon Middle School

***

"Staff, thanks for coming so quickly," Mrs. Marsh
spoke as her assistant principals gathered around her
conference table.   She stood tall in her red, stiletto heels.
Her matching pinstriped power suit hugged every curve of
her body. The brown specks in her Prada eyeglasses
reflected the brown in her eyes.

"Take one and share with the others," she said as
she handed the stack to Malcolm Dowell.

Malcolm quickly grabbed one of the packets,
separated the stacks, passed a couple across the table and
the rest to the person sitting next to him.

"This will be quick," said Mrs. Marsh. She gave
everyone a moment to receive their packet and then she
spoke. "As you know, our attendance rate was the only
thing that allowed us to make AYP last year.   Just in case
our test scores are not up to snuff—and if you flip through
the packets and review last year's scores—the odds are

they will not be up to snuff again. In that case, we are really going to need to count on attendance again. With that in mind, I need you to closely watch, as in, not give out any suspensions. If our students are in ISS or OOS, that counts against our attendance. We need to give more warnings. Our teachers need to give more warnings." She walked around the room, her heels click-clacking on the tiles.

"How many warnings are appropriate?" Katie Pitts, the 8th grade principal asked. This was her first year at Vilyon and her first year as an assistant principal.

"If there is no blood and no licks exchanged, there can never be too many warnings," stressed Mrs. Marsh.

"But," responded a shocked Katie, "that can be too time consuming for a teacher. What if the student is constantly disrupting a teacher's class so much that the teacher can't teach?"

"If the class is properly managed, then the student

should not have time to disrupt the class. If that is the reason for the write-up, then the teacher should be written up because that teacher is not managing his or her classroom." Mrs. Marsh smirked, an arrogance punctuated by red lipstick.

Katie could not believe what she was hearing or the simple fact that none of the other administrators seemed appalled by Mrs. Marsh's response. Principals were supposed to support their teachers, not allow them to be abused.

Mrs. Marsh stared angrily at Katie. "Are there any other questions?"

Katie did not respond.

"Anyone else?" Marsh stared around the room.

"Nope," Mr. Martin responded quickly.

Nobody else spoke.

"Then that will be all," said Mrs. Marsh. "Let's go back out and support our staff."

***

From: Shawna White/Vilyon Middle School/TCPS

To: Peter Pilsher

Re: After work

Welcome to Vilyon.   We're so glad you are here.   There's

a great bar and grill down the road that a lot of us frequent.

Would you like to join me there after a work, for a drink or

two—my treat?   I would love to properly welcome you to

Vilyon.   Let me know ASAP. Hope you can make it?

Shawna White

6th grade Math, Vilyon Middle School

***

Sticks and stone

do not break bones

still words sometimes hurt worse than bullets.

They are only children,

that is what the administrators say.

A teacher is an adult who should merely walk away.

***

From: Sarah Parks/Vilyon Middle School/TCPS

To: Laverne Anderson

Re: Support

Thanks for being my mentor this year. I really appreciate you going out of your way for me. I am sure I wear you out on a daily basis. And now I hate to admit it, but I'm already starting to burn out.   A student just called me "a fat bitch", and I took him to Ms. Johnson.   All she did was give him a verbal warning and a damn cookie.   What kind of support is that?   She said he needed to be in class to learn so he won't fall behind.   Now this kid is cussing me out every time he sees me in the hall.   What am I supposed to do?   If this is all he's going to get—a warning and a cookie—I might as well just buy a cookie jar and sit it on my damn desk.

Sarah Parks

7th grade Language Arts, Vilyon Middle School

***

From: Samuel Martin/Vilyon Middle School/TCPS

To: Certified Staff

Re: Field Trips

Due to budget cuts, field trips are being limited this year. There is one field trip per semester, per grade level. There is no maximum number of students allowed on the trip, but you must have enough students to cover the costs of your transportation and the admission fee of your event. Please remember that field trip permissions must be requested three months in advance. For the application packet, please see one of the clerks in the copy room. Your grade level administrator must approve the first fifteen pages of the application before the administrative team will review your application in its entirety. As always, field trips must coincide with the Vilyon Public School Academic Plan.

Thank you so much for keeping these guidelines,

Samuel Martin
Assistant Principal—Activities and Connections, Vilyon
Middle School

***

From: Laverne Anderson/Vilyon Middle School/TCPS

To: Sarah Parks

Re: Support

Hi Sarah! Sorry that you are having a rough day. I'm not sure what to say about the incident. Unfortunately at the end of the day, you just have to realize that you are on your own. But that offers some benefit to you as well. Your class is your own space. Take it and make it your home, and do not let anyone ever mess up your house. As for the student, later on, he will realize that he needs you more than you need him. Ignore him. Believe it or not, praise him instead of confronting him. Whatever it is; it's not about you. It's about him and something that he's not getting. Maybe you can be the one to give it to him. Maybe you will be the one to motivate him to become better than he is. On those days when you feel that you just can't do it anymore, please remember where my classroom

is; I'm here for you. Let's be sure and do dinner this week.

Laverne Anderson

7th grade Science, Vilyon Middle School

***

From: Peter Pilsher/Vilyon Middle School/TCPS

To: Shawna White

Re: After work

Shawna,

Thanks so much for the wonderful invite, but unfortunately

I am unable to join you this afternoon. Hopefully, I can

join you another time. Thanks again for the invite. It was

very kind of you.

Have an awesome day,

Peter Pilsher

6th grade Social Studies, Vilyon Middle School

***

From: Angela Williams/Vilyon Middle School/TCPS

To: Sonya Harte

Re: Field Trips

If you fill out my forms, I will fill out yours. These kids are definitely not going anywhere this year. Martin and Marsh are on the same crack pipe.

Angela Williams

8th grade Math, Vilyon Middle School

***

From: Sonya Harte/Vilyon Middle School/TCPS

To: Angela Williams

Re: Field Trips

My students will be taking field trips quite frequently this school year. Each day, my students will analyze the posters in the hallway as we walk to the cafeteria. At least once a month, we will explore the past, the present, and the future when we visit the Vilyon Middle School Media center. On a daily basis, my students can use their linguistic skills to decipher the meaning of the graffiti on the bathroom walls. Who could ask for anything more? Here at Vilyon, we provide the absolute best for our students. We are always striving to give our students a world-class education.

Sonya Harte

7th grade Social Studies, Vilyon Middle School

***

From: Alison Smith/Vilyon Middle School/TCPS

To: Certified Staff

Re: Library Visitation Schedule

We are currently updating our database and stocking our shelves with new books.   I will send out a visitation schedule as soon as we are done.   Until then, the media center is closed to both students and staff.

Also, please remember that you are not allowed to show videos or DVDs that do not come from the media center.

Thanks for your understanding,

Alison Smith

Media Specialist, Vilyon Middle School

***

From: Janet Wilson/Vilyon Middle School/TCPS

To: Faculty and Staff

Re: Free Drapes

My husband, Dr. Lawrence Wilson—Chief Cardiologist of Taylor County Hospital and I are currently redecorating our six bedroom home. With the economy not faring that well, I thought that some of you might be interested in having the old drapes I'm taking down. The drapes are dark chocolate brown and completely spot free, as we had them steam cleaned every other week. We are also giving away bed linens and rugs. First e-mail, first serve.

Janet Wilson

7th grade Math and Science Gifted, Vilyon Middle School

***

From: Tracey Peterson/Vilyon Middle School/TCPS

To: Shawna White

Re: Free Drapes

Well bless her heart. I'm so glad that we poor folks are lucky enough to be working in the same building as her. I tell you what—I've definitely been looking for some drapes and bed linens to redecorate my own house. How did she know? I've been searching above and beyond for something that has been right here all along.   Let me go get them right now. Us poor folks can't get our own stuff. New drapes are definitely number one on my priority list. It was right up there next to me paying my light bill. God bless you Mrs. Wilson and your doctor husband too.

Tracey Peterson

6th grade Language Arts, Vilyon Middle School

***

From: Shawna White/Vilyon Middle School/TCPS

To: Tracey Peterson

Re: Free Drapes

Girl, you are going to get into so much trouble one day.

Until then, I'll keep laughing.   How is your day going

now?

Shawna White

6th grade Math, Vilyon Middle School

From: Harold Jones/Vilyon Middle School/TCPS

To: Sonya Harte

Re: Recruiting Barack Voters

Hi Friend! My day is crazy. You know these 8th graders are off the chain as usual. Some things never change.   But I still had time to write my best buddy to make sure that she isn't killing anyone. I also wanted to know if you are willing to help me promote Obama.   It's time for a change girl, and I know he's going to do it for us.   Are you in?

Harold Jones

8th grade Social Studies, Vilyon Middle School

***

From: Sonya Harte/Vilyon Middle School/TCPS

To: Harold Jones

Re: Recruiting Barack Voters

You didn't even have to ask. You know that I jumped on the bandwagon a long time ago. Have you not seen my car lately? I probably have one hundred Obama stickers plastered all over my bumper. Let's get started. I'm all about change. Somebody needs to fix this messed up place, and I know Obama can do it. Are you going to send out an e-mail or something? Perhaps all those interested can get together this week after work at Island Breeze. I'll even pay for one drink for everyone. You can't take it with you after all.

Thanks for helping to change the world. I love you friend.

Sonya Harte

7th grade Social Studies, Vilyon Middle School

***

From: Harold Jones/Vilyon Middle School/TCPS

To: Sonya Harte

Re: Recruiting Barack Voters

I'm going to send out an e-mail in a couple of minutes.

Just had to break up a fight. These kids and their drama.

Sometimes I seriously wonder if education should be

completely free, but anyway, I will tell you about it later.

Harold Jones

8th grade Social Studies, Vilyon Middle School

***

From: Gerald Smith/Vilyon Middle School/TCPS

To: Faculty and Staff

Re: Copy Paper

I cannot believe that I'm writing this e-mail. This is something I would expect to have to say to our students but not to our teachers. Just a few moments ago, I placed a ream of copy paper in each staff member's mailbox. Now, staff members are coming to me, saying their paper is not in their mailboxes. It is a sad day when teachers and clerical staff steal from each other. Is it really that serious? Do we need to place a camera in the mailroom to monitor ourselves? Just think about what you're doing. Treat others as you would like to be treated. Unfortunately, I do not have any extra copy paper for those of you who have empty mailboxes.

Gerald Smith

Supply Manager, Vilyon Middle School

***

From: Harold Jones/Vilyon Middle School/TCPS

To: Faculty and Staff

Re: It is time for a change

Hello my fellow Americans and our wonderful international teachers. Today is a new era in our lives. It's a time for change. A time of change for us as parents, teachers, and comrades against ignorance and denial. Change, you say? Yes, change! I understand that you're looking out in the world and saying you do not see any change at this time, and you're right because we're not there yet. I'm asking you to help change come about, to be a part of the change.

There is a new knight in town, and he hails from the great state of Illinois. He talks to us about taking our country back from those who threaten us both socially and economically. He has dared to remind us that we are the

United States of America, and that by working together, we can be successful in all that we do.

That man is our future president of the United States, Senator Barack Obama. Even though I find it hard to believe, that in this strange day and age where the current government continues to do the same thing over and over again even though it does not work, that there are some people who do not know who Obama is and what he stands for, I must acknowledge that some people don't know him.

This is something that you and I working together, can change. Will you join me? Will you be there when this man of change, this man for the people, this man of the people, will take his inaugural oath and put this country's best foot forward? Will you be there?

If you are interested in being a part of the "Elect Obama" campaign, please join us on Thursday afternoon at 5pm at

Island Breeze.   You will receive one complimentary

beverage of your choice.

Do more than think about it?   Be a part of it.

Harold Jones

8th grade Social Studies, Vilyon Middle School

***

From: Margaret Bascombe/Vilyon Middle School/TCPS

To: Faculty and Staff

Re: Flu shots

Yes—we will be providing flu shots on campus again this year for our faculty and staff. Please place the date October 28 on your calendar. Because we want to make sure that everyone can afford these important medicinal aids, we are only charging $25.00 per shot. For your convenience, the shots will be offered on campus before and after school. I am also willing to accept post-dated checks for payment.

They say the flu is going to be awful this year, and we know how much you hate to be out of the classroom. Do not delay. Reserve your flu shot today.

Margaret Bascombe

School Nurse, Vilyon Middle School

***

From: Alicia Marsh/Vilyon Middle School/TCPS

To: Faculty and Staff

Re: Politics at school—please read

Dear Faculty and Staff,

Just a few moments ago, I read an e-mail that troubled me

greatly because it was regarding politics. Although I do

encourage you to become involved in politics—after all this

is your country—I do not encourage you to get involved at

work.

Your personal political opinions are your own, and they

should not be shared with your fellow staff members or our

student body. Please do this during your own time. From

8:30 to 4:30, you are on Vilyon County time.

As a reminder, school e-mail should not be used for the

transmittal of any information that is not used for

instructional purposes (this includes both social and

political). Violators will not receive warnings and will immediately be subject to referral and the loss of their laptop and desktop.

If you have additional comments, please see your grade level or area administrator ASAP.

Alicia Marsh

Principal, Vilyon Middle School

***

From: Alicia Marsh/Vilyon Middle School/TCPS

To: Faculty and Staff

Re: A good veterinarian

Hello Friends,

My husband just called and told me that our precious baby,

Lady, threw up on the carpet.   Since we just got Lady, we

still have not found a good veterinarian to care for her.

Please e-mail me if you know the name of a good

veterinarian.

On a different note, my daughter is selling calendars and

popcorn for her Adventure Troop. I will place the order

form in the mailroom.

Thank you for your continued support,

Alicia Marsh

Principal, Vilyon Middle School

P.S—God Bless John McCain and the Republican Party

***

From: Sonya Harte/Vilyon Middle School/TCPS

To: Harold Jones

Re: Marsh

Is insane.

Sonya Harte

7th grade Social Studies, Vilyon Middle School

***

From: Shawna White/Vilyon Middle School/TCPS

To: Tracey Peterson

Re: Marsh

Told you she was doing drugs. If only she had ate that

lasagna I made for her instead of giving it to her precious

Lady, things would be so different now.

Shawna White

6th grade Math, Vilyon Middle School

***

From: Harold Jones/Vilyon Middle School/TCPS

To: Sonya Harte

Re: Marsh

Hey, do not tell her she is insane.   She thinks she has

everyone fooled.   This e-mail will burn after being read.

Go Obama!

Harold Jones

8th grade Social Studies, Vilyon Middle School

***

From: Tracey Peterson/ Vilyon Middle School/TCPS

To: Shawna White

Re: Marsh

Hi! Do you really know where she lives? I heard her house is very, very nice.

Best Wishes,

Tracey Peterson

6th grade Language Arts, Vilyon Middle School

***

From: Shawna White/Vilyon Middle School/TCPS

To: Tracey Peterson

Re: Marsh

I heard it was nice too, but I have never been there. Somebody told me that it was in the Cedarville Golf Community. Her dad and the superintendent are seen there all the time playing golf together.

As for seeing her outside of school, I certainly have no interest in seeking her out in my spare time, not even to poison her. You know I don't even like seeing her at work.

Shawna White

6th grade Math, Vilyon Middle School

***

From: Tracey Peterson/ Vilyon Middle School/TCPS

To: Shawna White

Re: Marsh

You've actually seen her at work? That's a first. A real, honest to goodness Marsh sighting. What does she look like? LOL. All I have ever seen are the e-mails, and you know you can send those from home now. Maybe Marsh doesn't even exist. Perhaps, it's a government conspiracy to drive us all crazy. Anyway, I guess I need to take the kids on a restroom break. Damn heathens—like there aren't any trashcans in my room.

Best Wishes,

Tracey Peterson

6th grade Language Arts, Vilyon Middle School

***

They will tell you to look deeper

in search of the child who is really there.

Ignore the one who isn't real…

the one who speaks so coldly

the one who calls you names

who flips you the finger

when she thinks you're not watching

the one who stabs you in the front, not in the back

because seeing your face increases the pleasure.

But here's the scary thought: what if what you see is

all there is to see?

Do you stop trying

or do you continue to hope

that you will be the one

to make the difference?

***

From: Sally Walker@hotmail.com

To: Peter Pilsher/Vilyon Middle School/TCPS

Re: My son, Jeremy Walker

Dear Mr. Pilsher,

Since I was unable to attend the open house, I just wanted to take this opportunity to introduce myself to you and let you know a little more about Jeremy. I think that Jeremy can only be successful in an environment where the teachers know who he is. With that in mind, please forward this e-mail to your teammates as well. I'm sending it to you because the front office told me that you are his homeroom teacher.

First of all, Jeremy can be a little talkative at times in a classroom situation. He does not mean anything by it, but I think it comes from being an only child and with his father and me both working so much. Usually, if you tell

Jeremy to be quiet, he will respond after the third or fourth warning.

Secondly, Jeremy doesn't like to study at all. He also has a problem completing his homework, which is why his fifth grade teachers said that he had to stay in the fifth grade for two years. Jeremy's father and I are working on his bad habits this year. We have promised him a Wii and two hundred dollars if he makes all D's or higher this semester. Please give him extra credit to help him meet his goal.

Lastly, Jeremy is having some kind of psychological issue. I always forget what the therapist says, but Jeremy, without thinking about it, sometimes takes his privates out and fondles himself. I realize that some people think that Jeremy may belong in a special class, but he does not because he is actually very smart, just unmotivated. Therefore, his father and I will not consent to any special testing so please don't contact us about this. If you could talk to Jeremy ASAP about a signal that you can use to let him know that he is behaving inappropriately in class that would be greatly appreciated. This is a part of his IEP so you don't want to ignore it. Also, please be sure and sign Jeremy's daily progress report each day. I will sign it and return it to you on a regular basis.

If you have any questions, please do not hesitate to write me.

Thanks for all your help,

Sally Walker

***

From: Leslie Longmire/Vilyon Middle School/TCPS

To: Certified Staff

Re: Tissue in sinks

Dear teachers,

In order to cut down on the flooding in the restrooms—

which is caused by students stuffing the drain with tissue

paper and then turning the water on high—we are asking,

once again, that teachers do not allow students to have

individual restroom breaks except in the case of dire

emergencies. Basically, you need to see something

dripping or hear it dropping before you send the students to

the restroom unattended. Not only are the students wasting

tissue paper when they are in the restrooms alone, but they

are also causing the members of my janitorial staff to take

time away from other important assignments. When you

take your class to the restroom (and you need to send me

the exact times of your daily restroom breaks so I can place it on a spreadsheet. This will help us to identify which class is leaving a mess in the restroom), please be sure and choose a reliable monitor for each class. This monitor's job is to check the restroom before and after your class leaves. If a mess is discovered in the restroom, and you have not reported it to me or one of my staff members, then I will ask Mrs. Marsh to place a complaint in your file. Teachers, when my staff goes into your classroom each day, we strive to leave it better than we found it. Please do the same for our restrooms.

Thanks for helping us keep Vilyon clean,
Leslie Longmire
Head Custodian, Vilyon Middle School

***

From: Peter Pilsher/Vilyon Middle School/TCPS

To: Sally Walker

Re: Jeremy Walker

Dear Mrs. Walker,

Thank you for your e-mail. I will forward a copy of your e-mail to my teammates. I am sure that if we work together, we can ensure that Jeremy has a successful sixth grade year. If you have additional concerns, please do not hesitate to write me again.

I look forward to learning from Jeremy this year,

Peter Pilsher

6th grade, Social Studies, Vilyon Middle School

***

From: Sarah Parks/Vilyon Middle School/TCPS

To: Gail Jenkins

Re: Tissue Paper Crisis—Call George W. Bush, will you?

That bitch is insane!   She acts like this is a national

emergency.   She really needs to get a life or something.

You know, I have never actually seen her with a mop or a

broom in her hand.   Does she even really work here?

Sarah Parks

7th grade Language Arts, Vilyon Middle School

***

From: Gail Jenkins/Vilyon Middle School/TCPS

To: Sarah Parks

Re: Tissue Paper Crisis—Call George W. Bush, will you?

Hey, she does have a valid point about the bathroom, but what does she expect us to do? If these kids are just that damn nasty, then they're just that damn nasty. This e-mail should be going to the parents not to us. We did not raise these kids; they did. If these were my children, I would have drowned them at birth.

Gail Jenkins

7th grade Science, Vilyon Middle School

***

From: Marcus Watts/Vilyon Middle School/TCPS

To: Peter Pilsher, Sandra Wyatt, Tammy Eigers

Re: Jeremy Walker

Hi Sandra, sexy pregnant lady,

Have you found the father of those babies, yet? I still say they ain't mine—LMAO. The reason I'm writing is a very serious one. I just read your email about Jeremy, the porn magazines and his recreational activity in your class. Which magazines did he have?   With the economy going bad, I have not been able to keep up my monthly subscriptions, and if I can get them from him for free, then that works for me. Let me know, all right?

Marcus Watts

6th grade Science, Vilyon Middle School

***

From: Sandra Wyatt/Vilyon Middle School/TCPS

To: Peter Pilsher, Marcus Watts, Tammy Eigers

Re: Pervert!

You are a strange man Marcus! Stay away from him Peter. His own wife doesn't even like him. Marcus, do not try and take Peter over to the dark side. We like him nice and sweet just the way that he is. And Marcus, by the way, they were both *Dig Guys* magazines. Can you believe he actually came in here with gay porn? I will make sure you get them before the end of the day Marcus. I'm sure you will enjoy. ROFL!

Sandra Wyatt

6th grade Math, Vilyon Middle School

***

From: Peter Pilsher/Vilyon Middle School/TCPS

To: Tracey Peterson, Marcus Watts, Tammy Eigers

Re: Jeremy Walker

You all are hilarious. Tracey, until we come up with a way to deal with Jeremy, I have no problem with him doing his work in my classes if this is okay with everyone. He behaved well in my room. Hopefully, we will be able to meet with our assistant principal soon to discuss this issue. Let this not ruin our day. Talk to you all later.

Peter Pilsher

6th grade, Social Studies, Vilyon Middle School

***

From: Alicia Marsh/Vilyon Middle School/TCPS

To: Faculty and Staff

Re: Welcome our new Staff Members

Dear Friends,

Please welcome two new staff members to our team. If you have seen a tall, handsome man with glasses and gray streaks of wisdom in his dark hair, then you have already seen Carey Robinson. I have known Carey for many years, and he is a wonderful man who is transferring to our school from the Fulton County Public School System. Carey will be acting as our Assistant Principal in charge of Textbooks and Technology.

The other new addition to the team is April Simmons. April is coming to our school from the Detroit Public School System, and she has been in education for over twenty years. April is here to assist you as our Assistant Principal of Curriculum and Instruction. Again, please welcome our two new staff members. Let us make them a part of our happy home.

Alicia Marsh

Principal, Vilyon Middle School

***

From: Katy Holmes/Vilyon Middle School/TCPS

To: Faculty and Staff

Re: Sub Process

Good morning. Since many of you are new this year, I am writing to remind you of the sub procedures for Vilyon Middle School. Of course, you should have read about this process in your employee handbook, but just in case you did not, hear it goes.

First and foremost, you are responsible for finding your own subs, even during emergencies. If you are unable to do it, please make sure an immediate family member has a list of subs so they can find one for you. The only exception is when an administrator asks you to attend staff development training.

Once you secure your sub, please call and leave a message at the front office with your name and the name of your sub. If you are unable to find a sub, unfortunately you will need to come to work. At no time will classes be combined.

Any teacher who does not find a sub and does not show up for work will receive a formal referral, which will be placed in his/her personnel file. An accumulation of formal referral may interfere with transfer requests as well as the terms of an employee's contract.

If you have additional questions, please refer to your employee handbook.

Katy Holmes

Administrative Assistant to the Principal, Vilyon Middle School

***

From: Alicia Marsh/Vilyon Middle School/TCPS

To: Faculty and Staff

Re: Saying goodbye

Dear Friends,

Unfortunately, due to budget cuts, some of our staff members are being displaced. Please rest assured that Vilyon County will find other positions for these people as soon as possible.   The people that we are sad to see go are Alex Rodriguez from the cafeteria staff, Liu Shiang from the custodial staff, and Mary Lyons from the copy room. Additionally, the following teachers are also being displaced: Alexis Hall, Margaret Simmons, Keisha Bradley, Thomas Wilkinson, Mary Cavanaugh, Lisa Daniels, Paul Alexander, Simone Lexington, and Michelle Beechum.

For those of you who are concerned about your own positions, rest assured that no other staff members will be displaced this academic school year. However, there will be deeper budget cuts next year, and we will have a smaller staff as a result of the budget cuts. But that is in the future. Now, we must deal with the present because we cannot prepare our students for the future if they cannot handle the present.

With that in mind, please know that a few of your classes will increase in size, although no teacher will have more than 30 students. Your classrooms will also now be cleaned every other day, so please urge your students to clean up after themselves. Since Mary is leaving the copy room, teachers are now responsible for producing their own copies. The copy room will be open one hour before work and one hour after work. It will also be open during each grade level's planning period and from 9:30 to 10:20 for connections teachers. Please remember to make copies days in advance so that you will be prepared in case of a technical emergency.

Remember, it is all about the kids,

Alicia Marsh

Principal, Vilyon Middle School

***

From: Angela Williams/Vilyon Middle School/TCPS

To: Sonya Harte

Re: Saying Goodbye

Bullshit!   Bullshit! Bullshit!

Angela Williams

8th grade Math, Vilyon Middle School

***

From: Sharon Simmons/Vilyon Middle School/TCPS

To: Katy Holmes

Re: Sub Process

Hi Kitty Kay!

How is it hanging?   Please tell Mrs. Marsh that I might be dead tomorrow. It will be something that comes across slowly in the night, without warning, a definite emergency. Before I go to bed though, I will be sure to have my husband and my two little boys each show me their invaluable copies of the Vilyon Middle School Substitute list. If I am dead, I'm sure that finding a substitute for me will be the number one priority on their list.   An additional question: let us just say that my entire family except for my dog dies in the fire—should I be proactive and teach him how to use his paws in order to find a substitute to replace me?

By the way, thanks for keeping us current on the sub policies.

Sharon Simmons

Physical Education Teacher, Vilyon Middle School

***

From: Katy Holmes/Vilyon Middle School/TCPS

To: Sharon Simmons

Re: Sub Process

Hey girl! Do not shoot the messenger. I do not come up with these things. I just send out the e-mails. And don't worry, if you call me right before your house is completely burned down (yes forget about saving the children, call me instead), I will try and find you a sub. That is way too much pressure on the dog. Please remember though that if I cannot find you a substitute, you will receive a formal referral in your personnel file. I will make sure to have a copy permanently etched on your headstone. Have a great day.

Katy Holmes
AA to the Principal, Vilyon Middle School

***

From: Sonya Harte/Vilyon Middle School/TCPS

To: Angela Williams

Re: Saying Goodbye

Calm down girl; I completely agree. I'm really going to

miss some of those people, and I feel bad for most of them.

What if they don't get placed right a way? Simone's

husband lost his job two months ago, and they have five

kids. This displacement stuff is really hurting everyone.

Sonya Harte

7th grade Social Studies, Vilyon Middle School

***

From: April Simmons/Vilyon Middle School/TCPS

To: Certified Staff

Re: ESOL Program

Hello Most Excellent Teachers,

I'm writing to let you know that Vilyon is taking a new and better position as far as our ESOL programs. Beginning tomorrow, our fulltime ESOL program will be dissolved and our ESOL students will be included in our regular classes. Statistics have shown that "sink or swim" works better. Students learn better through socialization and not through exclusion. ESOL students will be scattered throughout the school in various classes depending upon their test scores. Some teachers will receive students who unfortunately do not speak a word of English. These students will be specifically placed in your class because your class roster indicates that you have one or more students who share that student's language.

Teachers, I know it sounds like a monumental task, but it can be done. As exceptional teachers, I know that you already use lesson plans, which appeal to the cultural diversity of our school. With our school population consisting of 50% minority students, working full-time with ESOL students will come naturally to all of you.

Although we will not have any ESOL teachers on staff any more, we will have a part-time ESOL coach, Florence Brown, who can work with you on a limited basis to make sure that all your students progress at grade level.

Florence is here to help you. Please utilize her.

I look forward to working with you,

April Simmons, Assistant Principal—Curriculum and Instruction, Vilyon Middle School

***

From: Angela Williams/Vilyon Middle School/TCPS

To: Sonya Harte

Re: Saying Goodbye

It's not enough to say goodbye when we're saying it

because of some bullshit.   We have budget cuts, but we

still have two new administrators.   An administrator of

textbooks and technology? You have got to be kidding me.

Curriculum and instruction?   Isn't that what teachers do

anyway? At least we try and instruct our students. We

hired two new administrators and let go of nine teachers.

Most of them have families to feed.   That is sickening.

Now, we have seven administrators who won't do anything

except take long lunch breaks.

And some of us might get extra students, but I can barely

keep the twenty-seven I have in-line now. In between

making my own copies, cooking lunch for the entire school

(the next thing they will be asking us to do), and cleaning

the restrooms, when am I supposed to be left alone to plan and to teach? It's getting to the point that I have started planning my sick days, weeks ahead of time.

Who's being left behind again? Thanks to all the people who make educational policies without teaching in today's classrooms first.

Angela Williams
8th grade Math, Vilyon Middle School

***

From: Florence Brown/Vilyon Middle School/TCPS

To: Certified Staff

Re: ESOL Program

Good morning fellow instructors!

I'm writing to let you know I'm available to help you with

any and all ESOL needs on Mondays, Wednesdays, and

Fridays from 7:30am to Noon. Please e-mail me to

schedule a meeting. Also, because there is one of me and

so many of you, please make sure that you have checked

out my webpage for ESOL FAQs before scheduling a

meeting. Time is one of our greatest assets. We need to

treasure it and use it wisely.

I'm here when you need me.

Florence Brown, ESOL COACH—Vilyon Middle School

***

Meetings before and after work.

Mandatory meetings during work.

Technology meetings about things we'll never use.

Data meetings, crammed with numbers and spreadsheets,

that mean nothing.

At the end of the day, we can tell if our students are

learning without meetings and technology.

Can he read at grade level or higher?

Can she convert fractions to decimals?

Can he locate countries he may never visit on a map?

Can she identify the seven levels of classification?

Can he explain the difference

between a subject and a predicate?

Can she respond to a writing prompt

with ease and correctly?

If not...instead of wasting our time at endless meetings,

Give us time to prepare to teach.

Only then will our goals be within reach.

***

From: Alicia Marsh/Vilyon Middle School/TCPS

To: All Certified Staff

Re: Exciting Staff News

Dear Friends,

I'm so excited to be able to share this news with you. It's regarding a wonderful staff development opportunity that's going to make it so much easier for us to achieve our goal of nurturing the whole student. This is a program which will remind us to take a step back and ask ourselves how we like to be treated. Many of you have read the book, and now we're going to live it.

Love & Discipline—Yes, they can go together. This is the acclaimed book by psychologists Andrew Lever and Sally Lever. The book has sold over five million copies and has been used successfully in schools all over the country.

Not only will each staff member be getting a copy of this wonderful book (via checkout in the media center), but both Dr. Levers will be coming in twice this year to spend the day with us. They will be attending our faculty and planning meetings and making classroom visits. They will share their ideas with us and help us all become better educators. This is such a great thing for us. Normally the Levers charge over $100,000.00 for school visits, but because I went to school with Sally, she and her remarkable husband are only charging Vilyon Middle School half their regular fee.

Are you as excited as I am? Get ready for *Love & Discipline*.

Our first meeting with the Levers will be next Friday morning. Please arrive at 7:30am. This is earlier than our usual faculty meetings, but I know that once we began our discussion, you will forget about the time.

Thanks for helping make Vilyon a remarkable place,

Alicia Marsh

Principal, Vilyon Middle School

***

From: Marcus Watts/Vilyon Middle School/TCPS

To: Sandra Wyatt

Re: Love & Discipline

Is that how you got your baby honey?   You and your husband playing a little Love and Discipline at home? ROFL.   If he doesn't tie you up at night, do you write him a referral and spank his butt? Love and Discipline. What rubbish?   I think Marsh has been in the field for way too long.   Forget the love. We just need to bring on the discipline.   You bring your paddle and I'll bring mine. Smack that!

Marcus Watts

6th grade Science, Vilyon Middle School

***

From: Sandra Wyatt/Vilyon Middle School/TCPS

To: Marcus Watts

Re: Sicko

Seriously Marcus,

If you were not my husband's best friend, I would have beaten the shit out of you a long time ago. You are such a sicko. Stop sending e-mails and try actually teaching for a change. Your students might actually pass a test. Oh, but then again, maybe not—they would need a real teacher for something like that. ☺

Sandra Wyatt

6th grade Math, Vilyon Middle School

***

From: Samuel Martin/Vilyon Middle School/TCPS

To: 930 Certified Staff

Re: Teacher Luncheon

Dear Teachers,

Please know that all the work you do each day is greatly appreciated. You are the wind beneath the wings of our students. Without you, this school could not exist. Therefore, it is with great regret I must announce that due to budget cuts, we will not be having our teacher appreciation lunch this year. Still know that you are appreciated more than words can say. Please enjoy the Vilyon coffee mugs which have been placed in all your mailboxes.

Samuel Martin

Assistant Principal—Activities and Connections, Vilyon Middle School

***

From: Angela Williams/Vilyon Middle School/TCPS

To: Sonya Harte

Re: Love & Discipline

Not going to say one word. Not a single word. I'm just going to sneak outside and smoke a cigarette.

Angela Williams

8th grade Math, Vilyon Middle School

***

From: Sonya Harte/Vilyon Middle School/TCPS

To: Angela Williams

Re: Love & Discipline

Good.

Sonya Harte

7th grade Social Studies, Vilyon Middle School

***

"How's it going, Harold?" Angela asked when she saw the skinny red-haired man emerge from behind the huge green trash bins.

Harold shrugged. "Nothing a new job can't help. Got a light?" he asked as he pulled a crumpled cigarette out of his pocket.

"Yeah." Angela removed a green lighter from her slacks pocket and held it out to him.

"Thanks," he said after taking a long drag. "It's been one of those days already. Damn kids. Caught some of the boys in the restroom having a pee contest on the walls. I'm foreseeing an e-mail from Leslie any minute now."

Angela snickered and took a puff of her cigarette. "You won't get an e-mail. She'll just bring a bucket and a rag and tell you to have at it. Haven't you read your contract? That part about *other duties as assigned.* If not, please see an administrator or refer to your employee handbook."

Harold laughed. "You have her down pat, don't you?"

Angela shook her head. "Not really. But after you hear the same shit every day, you start to learn it. This is your first year at Vilyon, right?"

"Fifth year teaching but first year here."

Angela looked at him thoughtfully. "How did you end up in this place?"

"Close to home and tired of driving," he said quickly. "It used to take me an hour each way to get to school and home. Now, I'm home in like fifteen minutes, ten minutes if traffic is good. You can't beat that. For that, I'm willing to put up with some of the crap I see around here."

"Definitely saving the money on gas. But the crap, I'm not sure about that. Sometimes, it seems like we're nose deep in it at Vilyon." Angela flicked the ash of her cigarette.

"Sometimes," Harold agreed. "Marsh is a character. I can't believe her response to my Barack e-mail."

"Well believe it," Angela said angrily. "And get used to it. She's a favorite at the County office so we're stuck with her until she quits or dies. Some of us have bets on which will happen first."

***

From: Angela Williams/Vilyon Middle School/TCPS

To: Sonya Harte

Re: Love & Discipline

But since you twisted my arm and the cigarette didn't help, I'm going to say something. Love & Discipline. This school is exactly like a prison—thousands of convicts and only a few guards. Who needs love in a place like this? $50,000. How many teachers did we lose again? And then Martin—that doofus—should be in charge of Special Education since he is so damn special. He took away our teacher luncheon and early release day. That's the only thing we had to look forward to this semester. What a crock of shit! This means mutiny. One of these days, I'm seriously going to pack up my shit and not come back. If the economy was any better, I wouldn't be here today.

I did get to spend some time with Harold Jones on my break though. He's a good guy.

Angela Williams

8th grade Math, Vilyon Middle School

***

Some lose their jobs,

some simply want to sit on their butts all day.

They live

for a teacher's favorite two words—

June and July.

Some don't even know what they teach,

but claim they are teachers.

Thank goodness for those who actually care.

***

"Michael," Mrs. Morgan called when she saw him walking towards the media center. He kept walking. His pants were too large and falling off his body, exposing red-and-blue checked boxers. Kids these days. "Michael, can I speak to you for a moment," she said in a calm voice.

Damn, Michael thought as he turned around. I'm not even in her class now, and she's still bothering me.

Mrs. Morgan waited for Michael to approach before she spoke; she was very much aware of the other kids who were walking in the hallway. She double-checked her watch before speaking. "Aren't you supposed to be in your Science class now?"

"I am," he said in a snappy tone as he glanced down at his sneakers. She was always nagging him.

"In the sixth grade hallway, Michael?"

"Mr. Peterson sent me to pick up something."

Mrs. Morgan stared at him. She knew he was lying.

"Where is your pass then?"

Michael shrugged. "Guess I must have dropped it."

"Michael," Mrs. Morgan said with a loud sigh. "You're only going to get so many chances. And this one is going to be the last one. Go back to class now, and I'm going to pretend I never saw you instead of writing you up as AWOL."

Michael hunched up his shoulders. "I don't care. So what if you write me up? Ain't nothing gonna happen anyway. You need to check yo' self with those crusty yellow teeth and that bad breath and back up off me. This is the last chance I'm going to give you."

"Michael," Mrs. Morgan gasped as she placed her hand over her mouth. She could not believe what he was saying. She reached out to grab his arm, but he jerked away. "Michael, what's wrong? This is not the boy I had a few years back in sixth grade. What has happened to you?"

"I've warned you lady," Michael said as he instinctively placed his free hand under his shirt near where a gun rested in his pants. "Don't touch me. You're about to start something."

"Excuse me." Principal Simmons walked by. "I'm sure there's not a problem here, is there?"

"No ma'am," Michael said quickly. "I was just heading back to class. Thanks Mrs. Morgan," he said as he swaggered away. I could've killed them both, he thought. Bang, bang, dead.

"Good," the principal said as she stood with Mrs. Morgan. They watched as Michael walked in the opposite direction of his class.

Mrs. Morgan wrung her hands together. "He is AWOL. He's not going back to class. He should not even be on this hallway." Her heart thumped in her ears.

"Don't worry," Principal Simmons said, "he obviously needs to let off some steam. I don't think he's a danger to anyone. Our cameras are monitoring the grounds, and if he attempts to leave campus, we'll stop him. Let's not create a problem when there isn't one."

"Maybe, you can take him to the counselor, though," suggested Mrs. Morgan. "I just feel that something is not right with him. Maybe she can get him to open up."

Principal Simmons placed a hand on Mrs. Morgan's back. "Let's not worry about this Louise. I told you everything is fine. Go back to your class and enjoy your planning period. I know your Academic Goals for the year are due tomorrow. Let's make sure you have those ready."

With that, Principal Simmons walked away, leaving Louise Morgan standing in the same spot, staring at her. Students raced by in a blur, their chatters echoing throughout the hallway.

***

From: Angela Williams/Vilyon Middle School/TCPS

To: Sonya Harte

Re: Starting my own school

Do you know what I would need to do in order to start my own school?   How did Ron Clark do it?   If I have a movie made about my life can I start my own school?   Maybe that's what I should do.   I need a place where I can teach without all the bullshit.   I love the kids, seriously I do, but it's the bullshit I can't stand.

Thanks for always being there for me girl and for listening to my bullshit.

Angela Williams

8th grade Math, Vilyon Middle School

***

From: Sonya Harte/Vilyon Middle School/TCPS

To: Angela Williams

Re: Your Own School

Well besides accreditation, licensure, and other teachers, there is one very important thing that I know you certainly do not have. MONEY! Sorry girl. Until we can get our own school, we just need to work on making this one as good as it can be. Suck it in and do the right thing. Together, WE CAN make a difference. Isn't that what Obama said? Yes, WE CAN.

Sonya Harte

7th grade Social Studies, Vilyon Middle School

***

From: Angela Williams/Vilyon Middle School/TCPS

To: Sonya Harte

Re: WE CAN

Watch those words you're typing. Don't use political phrases in your e-mail on Vilyon Middle School's time. During these eight or so hours (add 2 or 3 hours a day depending on how much additional work they throw at us), they own you body and soul. They control what you do and when you do it. They also control what you think and how you think about it. Politics that would allow a black man to be President is item number one on the "tyranny list" in the states of Georgia, Mississippi, and Alabama. Other items on the tyranny list include: Free Thinking, Creative Learning, and Equal Rights. Please stop. I would hate for you to suddenly be displaced. LOL.

Angela Williams

8th grade Math, Vilyon Middle School

***

From: Sonya Harte/Vilyon Middle School/TCPS

To: Angela Williams

Re: Yes You Can

There's my girl. Welcome back. You are excused from

your temporary loss of sanity. Since I'm one of your very

best friends, I will not even charge you for your therapy

session. I knew my psychology degree would be useful to

me some day. Please look for my bill in your employee

mailbox.

Sonya Harte

7th grade Social Studies, Vilyon Middle School

***

From: Alicia Marsh/Vilyon Middle School/TCPS

To: All Teachers

Re: Sitting on the job (Read immediately upon receipt)

Dear Teachers,

Please be reminded that as effective teachers you should never sit down when you have students in your class. Statistics show that teachers who sit down during their classes have a higher rate of discipline problems. As you teach, you should constantly be standing in a position where you can see all your students and they can see you or you should be walking among them. This encourages your students to focus on their learning and prevents classroom distractions. It also prohibits cheating in a testing environment. Teachers who are caught seated at their desks will receive a verbal reprimand on the first offense and a formal reprimand on the second offense.

If you feel poorly and are too unwell or tired to stand up and properly manage your class, perhaps you need to take a sick day. If this is the case, please refer once again to your employee handbook.

As always, thanks for keeping on your toes,

Alicia Marsh

Principal, Vilyon Middle School

***

From: Sandra Wyatt/Vilyon Middle School/TCPS

To: Marcus Watts

Re: On my ass

Man, Marsh is a bitch. She just came into my classroom, and I was sitting down with my swollen feet propped in a chair. It's not like the kids were doing anything but taking a pretest anyway. If they want to cheat on a pretest, then that's their stupid choice. It's not like I won't figure it out before the school year is over. Marsh is just evil. Hasn't she seen the extra twenty pounds I'm carrying around with me? The woman has no empathy genes in her body. I used to like her, but she has gone completely insane this year. She is the reason Roe vs. Wade came to be. Obviously her parents missed the memo.

Sandra Wyatt

6th grade Math, Vilyon Middle School

***

With one cruel look that promised bullying for the rest of the school year, Kelly cleared the back of the classroom so that she and Sheneice could eat their lunch in peace. Everyone else could kiss her ass. She made the rules around here.

Mrs. Valkrie frowned but did not say anything as the kids rearranged themselves for lunch. It was bad enough that she had to eat lunch in the room with her students, but she certainly wasn't going to get involved with Kelly Wyatt if the other kids did not insist upon it. She had already had Kelly as a student last year, and after her car tires had been slashed by Kelly's boyfriend—who although he admitted committing the crime, he had never been charged because of school safety reporting issues— she had learned to ignore Kelly as much as possible.

"So have you spoken to Mr. Myers yet?" Sheneice whispered as she leaned over towards Kelly.

"Not yet," replied Kelly in a sly voice, "but I will. I was thinking about staying after school today. That way it will just be me and him."

Sheneice's mouth fell open. "I wish I could be that cool. I'm too scared to do something like that."

Kelly shrugged. "It's no big deal. If he wants some of this, I'll give him some for an A. If he doesn't, and he gives me a hard time, then I'll just have to talk to him about what happened to Mr. Jackson. If he's smart, he'll take me up on my offer."

"I heard he was married though girl, and he wears that gold WWJD bracelet on his wrist."

"WWJD," Kelly repeated. "What does that mean?"

"What would Jesus do?"

"Jesus would have been different if he knew me," Kelly said with a laugh. "I could have gotten an A in his class too. Now I'm going to get an A for you too girl, just wait and see."

***

From: Jackson Myers/Vilyon Middle School/TCPS

To: Sarah Parks

Re: How's the other newbie?

Haven't seen you much since orientation? How are things going? I hope you're doing better than I am. I care—that's why I wanted to become a teacher, but these kids don't care. Is it normal to feel burnt out your first year?

The wife gave me permission to do Starbucks after work if you're game. Let me know if you're interested in a coffee chat.

Jackson Myers

8th Grade Language Arts, Vilyon Middle School

***

Test scores are low, very low.

In a meeting, the administrator asks

What went wrong?

And what did *I* do that didn't work?

Why does it have to be about me?

Perhaps, I actually did my job.

Perhaps, I stayed late after work to create exciting,
interactive plans.

Perhaps, I came in early and prepared with a fierce desire to
teach, to share.

Perhaps, I read my students the questions and the answers
to tomorrow's quiz.

Perhaps, just perhaps…

It's about the students and not about me.

Perhaps, they just don't care.

And eventually you realize

What worked for Ron Clark and Jaime Escalante

will not work for you.

Then you start to not care yourself.

***

From: Sarah Parks/Vilyon Middle School/TCPS

To: Jackson Myers

Re: How's the other newbie?

I have worked so hard that I don't feel like a newbie anymore. I'm now an experienced veteran, and I completely understand about the burnout stage. I can't believe I left real estate for this, even though I would be homeless now if I was still in real estate. Still, I don't think what we go through every day is worth it.

What we have to deal with—I don't know about you, but I sort of feel like the government is wasting money on most of these kids.

As for Starbucks, I'll be there.

Sarah Parks

7th grade Language Arts, Vilyon Middle School

***

From: Alicia Marsh/Vilyon Middle School/TCPS

To: All Certified Staff

Re: E-mails

Dear Faculty,

Please be sure and check your e-mail regularly throughout the day.   Sometimes, important information is sent out over the computer. Many parents also choose to communicate via the Internet. When they do so, please respond within two hours. The number of phone calls I receive each day regarding insufficient communication is astounding. As teachers, it is a part of your job to maintain frequent communication with the parents of your students. If you cannot respond to them, this means that you can't do your jobs. If this sounds unfamiliar to you, please refer to your employee handbook.

Alicia Marsh

Principal, Vilyon Middle School

***

From: Sonya Harte/Vilyon Middle School/TCPS

To: Angela Williams

Re: E-mails

So, can we sit down to respond to e-mails or do we have to stand up? It's very tedious typing when I'm standing. What if I have classes for three hours straight and I'm not supposed to be at my desk when I have a class? Oh the dilemma, the dilemma!

Sonya Harte

7th grade Social Studies, Vilyon Middle School

***

From: Jackson Myers/Vilyon Middle School/TCPS

To: Sarah Parks

Re: How's the other newbie?

I know what you mean, and it hurts. How long will it be

like this? I guess that's why they give us mentors. Mine is

a joke though. She basically told me to sink or swim and

not to bother her for the rest of the year. Thank goodness

for friendships. See you at Starbucks.

Jackson Myers

8th Grade Language Arts, Vilyon Middle School

***

From: Angela Williams/Vilyon Middle School/TCPS

To: Sonya Harte

Re: E-mail

I'm all in favor of staying in contact with parents. I would like to e-mail a few of them and personally thank them for ruining my life. These kids are insane. Half of my second period class (15 out of 30) do not know their multiplication tables, but gee, they're all on the Boys' basketball team. I wonder how they got promoted. Forget reading, writing, and arithmetic—all of that is old news.

If the Parent Support Center really wants to do something for us, then they should invite all of the parents to a Birth Control Seminar. They should give out free contraceptives in hopes that most of them will never reproduce again.

Angela Williams

8th grade Math, Vilyon Middle School

***

From: Alicia Marsh/Vilyon Middle School/TCPS

To: Charles Walker, II

Re: Phone Call

Dear Charles,

Please accept my sincere apologies for the phone call you received earlier from Ms. Pitts. Rest assured that Gavin is not being suspended today or any other day. Although Ms. Pitts is a wonderful person, she was unaware of the regard in which Gavin is held here at Vilyon. I tried to personally call you myself, but I was unable to reach you.

Please feel free to call me at anytime. As always, we thank you for your continued generosity towards our basketball and academic bowl teams.

Thanks for all you do,

Alicia Marsh

Principal, Vilyon Middle School

***

From: Alicia Marsh/Vilyon Middle School/TCPS

To: Katie Pitts

Re: Gavin Walker

Katie,

Thank you for following school protocol and calling Mr. Walker regarding the issue that occurred with Gavin and another student. Due to extenuating circumstances, I have cancelled the suspension you gave Gavin. Normally, students who fight on school property are suspended for at least three days, but Gavin's case is a special one because he's the captain on the basketball team. In the future, so that I may guide you, please submit all your suspension requests to me before you call the parents.

You're doing a great job. Keep it up.

Alicia Marsh

Principal, Vilyon Middle School

***

From: Sonya Harte/Vilyon Middle School/TCPS

To: Angela Williams

Re: E-mails

ROFL.   Just remember that your e-mails are sometimes

monitored (AKA—Big Sister is Watching You), and I'm

not sure if you receive unemployment compensation if you

get fired.

Still, you always keep me rolling.

Sonya Harte

7th grade Social Studies, Vilyon Middle School

***

Does racism exist in public education?

You have to be joking, right?

Just because a black man might be President of the US,

It doesn't mean the rules have changed.

Test scores don't always determine placement.

Skill sets and personalities are rarely matched with jobs.

Too often

it's the color of the skin

and the address where one lives

that answers all the questions.

***

From: Charles Walker II @blackberry.net

To: Alicia Marsh/Vilyon Middle School/TCPS

Re: Phone Call

Hi Alicia. Thanks for your e-mail. It's okay. You know that I'm quite fond of you and your programs. I plan on doubling my donations to your school this year, by the way. Have to support the children. Anyway, I also wanted to follow through on this thing with the other kid. Gavin called and told me that this Hispanic kid is always threatening to beat him up, which is the only reason he fought back. Hope this kid is getting suspended for quite a while.

Thanks for all you do,

Charles Walker Attorney at Law

Sent from my Blackberry

***

From: Katie Pitts/Vilyon Middle School/TCPS

To: Jack Lincoln - Superintendent of Schools, Vilyon County

Re: Two Weeks Notice

Dear Mr. Lincoln,

It is with the deepest regret that I hereby submit my two-week resignation notice for the 8th grade Assistant-Principal position at Vilyon Middle School. To be very honest, it is not what I assumed it would be. Having taught previously only at a private school, I am not prepared for Vilyon Middle School. Thank you for the opportunity.

Katie Pitts

Assistant Principal—8th Grade, Vilyon Middle School

***

Michael grabbed the apple off Jamal's plastic tray. "You know you aren't going to eat it anyway," he said before taking a big bite.

"I'm not going to eat that crap," Jamal said with a yawn. "I told that old bitch I didn't want it and I was just gonna throw it away, but she was like you have to have two sides, so I was like whatever. If they were giving away ice cream as a side, then it would be another story. She wouldn't have to tell me twice."

As Ms. Valkrie walked passed their table, Michael blurted, "Ms. Valkrie, why don't you turn on the television? We need something to do in here besides eat and look at these ugly girls." He stared in the direction where Kelly and Sheneice were sitting.

"Beep, beep, that must be the sound of my gaydar going off," Kelly yelled across the room at Michael. "You don't look at girls anyway. You save your eyes for when you and your homeboy, or should I say homegirl, Jamal are in the bathroom together."

"Ooh," a few students moaned before the entire class went silent.

"Punta," Jamal screamed as he rose to his feet. "You weren't saying that when you were sucking my dick last night."

Ms. Valkrie rushed over to Michael's table. "Girls and boys, let's try and get along. If you can't say anything nice, then don't say anything at all."

Kelly dashed across the room and stood inches from Jamal's face. "I got a dick for you," she hissed. "My boyfriend too. After school, he's gonna—"

Ms. Valkrie stood between the two of them. "Either you can end this now or I can get an administrator in here."

Michael stood up. "It's over," he said as he put a hand on Jamal's shoulder. "We'll deal with it later," he whispered to his friend.

Kelly shrugged. "Yeah, it's over," she said in a non-convincing tone before going back to her seat. She flipped Jamal the finger.

Once everyone was back in their seats, Ms. Valkrie turned on the television, and soon the class of eighth graders were debating which episode of SpongeBob was better.

But not all of the students were interested in SpongeBob. Jamal and Michael were busy carrying on their own conversation, and Kelly was occupied with texting her boyfriend, Juan. The situation was far from over.

***

From: Katie Pitts/Vilyon Middle School/TCPS

To: Anderson Pitts@emory.edu

Re: Two Weeks Notice

Dear Grandfather,

I'm not sure how to say this, but I realize that I'm not happy with my job. It's actually more of a deep dissatisfaction and depression than a simple unhappiness. If you're merely unhappy, I think you can deal with it. My problem is worse than that, and I've been thinking about it since this summer when I first started working in this position. I honestly do not feel that I'm making any kind of difference here at Vilyon. My dream has always been to inspire others. I do not believe I'm doing that here.

As a psychiatrist, you always challenge me to evaluate and reflect upon everything before I make a decision, and on this one, I have spent many a sleepless night, but I know this is the right decision for me.

One thing I remember you telling me is that if I do not believe in something I'm doing, then to not do it, especially if I have any doubts. My conclusion, which allowed me to make the decision to leave my job, is that I do not believe in free, public education as it is now (or as it exists at Vilyon Middle School). Unfortunately, I do not believe that all children deserve a free education, and I'm extremely pissed off that my tax dollars actually help pay for it.

In my opinion, children who don't want to learn and show no respect to others don't deserve an education or a free lunch for that matter. Did you know that at my school, 90% of the students receive a free or reduced-priced lunch, yet half of the food on their trays ends up uneaten and in the trash?

I still have two hours left to go in my day, and I have already been cussed out by eleven students and seven parents. Still I'm expected to merely grin and accept it all when I'm spoken to in a manner in which I wouldn't even speak to a stray dog. I'm also expected to let my teachers, who I'm supposed to support and defend, be treated in a similar manner so that parents will not withdraw their children from our school.

Ideally as a principal, I would encourage my students to accept responsibility for their actions so they can be as successful as they can be. If acceptance means suspension, then the rules are changed as our budget is based on attendance. As for rules, there is one set for one group and a different set up for the other group. The flexible, ever-changing, lenient rules are for those who are gifted, for those whose parents contribute either time or money to VMS, and for those who can bring fame to the school. The set-in-stone, no chances given rules are for those who could be gifted, for those whose parents can barely afford to dress them and/or barely speak English, and for those who bring notoriety to the school.

Even with that said, I still stand behind one of my earlier statements. Not all children deserve a free education. Grandfather, you are a famous psychiatrist, and there is even a wait list for people to see you. Yet we both know that you don't see everyone. You have even told some of your patients to keep their money and find another doctor because you could not help them because they were not ready. These people were even paying you money.

These students and their parents are not paying anything. They get free transportation, free meals, and free instruction, which the majority of them do not appreciate. Earlier this morning, I asked three students (one from each of the three grade levels) why they came to school, and I kept waiting for the answer that I wanted to hear.

Student 1: My mother said there is no one to keep me at home, and that you would watch me.

Student 2: Lunch and breakfast is free.

Student 3: My PO said I had to stay in school.

The right answer never came. Nobody told me that they were here because they wanted to learn and to be successful. Nobody said they were here to receive an education.

I believe that we are giving them something that most of them don't care about. Of course you can say that as children, they don't know any better, but their parents don't appreciate it either, not when they don't support the efforts of the educators who dedicate their lives to helping the children of strangers. In fact, the attitudes of the parents are generally worse than the attitudes of the students. I called a parent this morning and told her that her child was smoking in the restroom, endangering himself and possibly everyone at school. The parent hung up on me after telling me that from 8:30 to 4:30 her son was my problem.

In some countries, education is not free; even poor parents are expected to pay. But in those places, the students appreciate the instructions and those that provide it. Some of the students walk miles to sit in a one-room classroom with dirt floors. Sometimes there are no books, no dry erase boards—not even chalkboards—only the floors. Lunch is not provided, and some people don't eat all day. Parents sacrifice to pay for their children's educations. Because it costs so much, children do not fail, and they respect both their parents and their teachers. They realize the importance of education.

The same cannot be said for most families in the United States. People see education as a right— something they are entitled to—but that is not true. Education is a privilege, an honor. If it is not appreciated, it should be taken away.

Then the question arises, how many chances should be given? Even I must admit that answer is not easy. Perhaps it depends on the child and his/her actions. Unfortunately, I do not have the answers to many of the questions I'm posing to you in this letter.   All I can say is that I know I'm not where I should be right now, and as much as it hurts me to resign from my job, I have to do so in order to save myself.

I hope you can forgive me.   You have raised a family of educators, from my mother who was a teacher for over forty years, to Uncle Bob who was a principal for thirty years.   Both my brothers have also chosen education as their careers.   I really do not want to disappoint you, Grandfather. Please forgive me for not being strong enough.

Katie Pitts,
Assistant Principal—8th Grade, Vilyon Middle School

***

From: Alicia Marsh/Vilyon Middle School/TCPS

To: Alicia Fontaine

Re: Job Opportunity

Dear Alicia,

Hope all is going well for my nearest and dearest best

friend. I told you I would keep my eyes open for a job

since you were eager to get back into a school after a five-

year break. Well guess what? A position has come up,

and it's the perfect job. My eighth grade principal has just

resigned for personal reasons, emotional I think, and I need

a replacement ASAP. Unfortunately she just wasn't' cut

out for the position. Although I know you have not worked

as a principal before, you do have your leadership degree,

and since you've been teaching for fifteen years, there

won't be much that I will need to teach you. The best thing

is that you and I work like twin sisters, and you know how I like things. Please let me know if you want the job.   This would really make my day.

Love,

Alicia Marsh

Principal, Vilyon Middle School

***

"What's wrong baby?" Juan asked. His girlfriend's voice wavered on the other end of his Blackberry.

"I need you to come out with yo' boys and get these little faggots who disrespected me," Kelly said in a tearful voice as she talked quietly in a bathroom stall. Of course, she was faking the tears, but she knew Juan wouldn't risk showing up on school property without a good reason

Juan was twenty-one so he really didn't have a reason to be on campus. In fact, the last time he had arrived at school and tried to check out Kelly, the county police had locked him up for twenty-four hours. He didn't want to give the cops another reason to come after him and his drug business, so he avoided the school as much as possible.

"What you talking about?" Juan asked. He carefully straightened a line of coke on his coffee table with a credit card that did not bear his name.

"These two boys called me and my homegirl bitches, Juan. I know you ain't gonna let them get away with that."

Juan placed his face close to the table and snorted up the white line. "Damn baby," he sniffed, "you know I ain't feeling that, but I ain't trying to get caught up in that school starting no stuff."

"You didn't have no problem bothering me yesterday at my house when my parents went to the movie, but now you ain't got time for me. Forget calling me again." Kelly's voice grew cold. "My phone will be busy."

"Come on baby," Juan begged. Without Kelly he would lose out on some of his drug sales at Vilyon. "You know I love you."

"Whatever man," said Kelly. There was no way she was going to let Michael and Jamal get away with disrespecting her. If she let that happen, then the other kids would be all over her too. She was willing to lie to Juan if that was what it would take.

"If you don't care that Michael and Jamal are hanging with the Crips, and they are the ones who shot up your homey Jaime the other night, then that shows what kind of little boy you are."

Juan sat upright. His ears burned. "Those are the dudes who shot up Jaime and his old lady? Are you sure, Kelly?" He ran his finger along his nose.

"Yeah, I'm sure," Kelly lied, "but what's it to you?"

"You know better than that baby," Juan said quickly. "Nobody messes with one of my boys. Where can I find these two fools after school? Those little punks ride the bus, I bet."

Kelly smiled, checked to make sure her purple lip liner was on straight, and blew a kiss at herself in the bathroom mirror. "Love you, baby," she giggled.

***

From: Anderson Pitts@emory.edu

To: Katie Pitts

Re: I love you!

Dearest Katie,

Not in your entire life have you ever disappointed me. In fact, you have always inspired me by daring to question and never simply following orders. I believe in you. If you say this job is not right for you, then it isn't. Perhaps there is not an ideal job for you. In that case, I urge you to create it. Perhaps you need to start your own school centered on principles in which you can believe.

In your e-mail, you talked about schools around the world where learning occurs and is similarly respected. I urge you to go and visit one of these places. If you check your e-mail, you should see a Delta Airlines gift certificate I purchased for you a few moments ago—it will take you anywhere in the world you choose to go, for you to see

what makes these places work. Then, just maybe, you will

come back here and live your own dream.

I look forward to being a part of your dream.

Love Always,

GrandFather

Dr. Anderson Pitts, Emory Hospital

***

"Mr.Pilsher, may I come in?" a short dark skinned kid asked from the door of Peter Pilsher's room. The kid wore glasses and was dressed neatly with his jeans pulled up and his shirt tucked in, unlike most of his male peers.

"Of course you can come in Javier," Mr. Pilsher responded with a smile. He glanced down at his watch. It was 4:35. "Did you miss your bus or something?"

Javier walked nervously into the room. His steps seemed hesitant. "No, I didn'tttttt," he stuttered a little bit as he tried to control his accent. "I'm a bus rider. Anyway, I stayed because I wanted to check out some books from the media center, but it was closed."

Mr. Pilsher looked at him thoughtfully. "Have you read all the books you have at home?"

Javier held his head down sadly. "Mr. Pilsher, the only books I have at home are an old dictionary and a thesaurus, and I've read both of them front to back. My

Nana and I don't have extra money for books."

Mr. Pilsher glanced at Javier. Yes, he was dressed neatly, but his clothes had seen better times, and his sneakers were old and the stitches were beginning to show.

"Do you want to borrow some of my books? I have quite a few, and you're welcome to them anytime." Mr. Pilsher pointed to the two tall bookshelves in the back corner of the room. The shelves overflowed with books.

Javier's head jerked up. "You would let me do that? You don't even know me that well."

Mr. Pilsher rose from his desk and walked around to Javier. "I know enough about you," he said when he was within inches of his student. "I know that you come into my class every day with a polite greeting for everyone. I know that you're always focused on what you're supposed to be doing. I know you do your work the first time I ask you to, and you do it perfectly. That's all I need to know. Because of that, you can consider me to be your personal library."

Suddenly, Javier felt tears running down his face, and he covered his face with his hands. This was his third year in America, and none of his other teachers had ever been so nice to him.

"It's okay," Mr. Pilsher said to him and reached for the tissue box on his desk. "But let it out if you need to."

"Thank you, Mr. Pilllsher," Javier said in between sobs. "You are a very nice man, and it means more to me than you know." After a minute, he stopped sobbing and moved his hands away from his face. He removed his glasses and wiped his face with one of the tissues.

"You're an awesome young man, Javier," Mr. Pilsher told him, "and don't ever let anyone tell you otherwise. You're going to do big things."

Javier agreed with a nod. "I am," he said confidently. "I have to, for my family. My parents brought me here from Mexico so that I could get a good education and become a doctor and help out back home in my country."

"I've seen your permanent record Javier. You've gotten all As every year since you have been here. You're definitely getting a good education. I'm sure your parents are very proud of you."

"Yes in heaven, they are," Javier said. "They died in a car accident last year, but I never forget what they wanted for me, to make a better life for myself and my family still in Mexico."

Mr. Pilsher felt as though he were about to cry himself. "Get as many books as you like," he told Javier. "When you bring those back, you can get more."

Javier smiled.

"Oh," Mr. Pilsher asked, "do you have a library card to the Vilyon Public library?"

"No, I don't, but it's not far from my house. Nana doesn't get out much, and the librarian won't give me a card without an adult."

"Well," suggested Mr. Pilsher, "what if you call Nana after you pick out some books and let's see if she will give me permission to drive you to the library and get you a library card. We can't have a future doctor running out of books on the weekends, can we?"

Javier's smile grew even wider. "You're the best teacher ever, Mr. Pilsher. I hope you can be my teacher forever."

Mr. Pilsher returned the smile. Today, he felt like he had made a difference.

***

From: Alicia Marsh/Vilyon Middle School/TCPS

To: All Certified Staff, Counselors, and Administrators

Re: Bus Duty

Dear Staff,

The Taylor County Schools Bus Supervisor called me this morning to inform me that several of the bus drivers had a hard time keeping a few of our students in their seats and cooperative today. To avoid this on the return trip, we have been asked to place a few staff members on the afternoon school bus routes. These staff members will ride the buses with the students and then return to school.

I apologize for any imposition this may cause, but if you would please refer to your employee handbook on page 269, you will note that this is listed as a possible school day occurrence and is part of your job description as an educator.

All staff members will not be needed as chaperones are only being randomly placed on buses. Not all buses will be chaperoned; if you have a teammate who is being asked to chaperone one of the buses, please split their homeroom students on your team so that no student is left unsupervised. Chaperones should expect to return on campus no later than 6pm.

Below is the list of randomly selected staff members who will be chaperoning buses:

Katie Pitts, Angela Williams, Sonya Harte, Gail Jenkins, Harold Jones, Shawna White, Sharon Simmons, Jeremy Lazarsky, Sandra Wyatt, and Peter Pilsher.

Thanks for your help in supporting our bus drivers and keeping our students safe,
Alicia Marsh
Principal, Vilyon Middle School

***

From: Angela Williams/Vilyon Middle School/TCPS

To: Sonya Harte

Re: Why am I not surprised?

To see both our names on that damn list. I guess the bitch

can read.   Of course, I didn't see any administrators'

names on the list.   That would involve one of them

actually having to really deal with the students.

Angela Williams

8th grade Math, Vilyon Middle School

***

From: Sandra Wyatt/Vilyon Middle School/TCPS

To: Marcus Watts

Re: Bus Duty

Man I hate her. It's just what my big fat butt and I planned on doing this afternoon—riding a school bus home. Have you been on one of those buses lately? Those buses are not made for pregnant women. Hell, I don't even know how our students can sit comfortably in those seats.

Sandra Wyatt

6th grade Math, Vilyon Middle School

***

From: Sonya Harte/Vilyon Middle School/TCPS

To: Angela Williams

Re: Bus Duty

Oh well. At least, we'll be saying goodbye to the kids. If

we get lucky, we'll learn the exact locations of some of

their homes, and then we can do some drive-bys later on.

As far as the administrators, Pitts was the first name on the

list. I wonder what she did to get on Marsh's shit radar.

Sonya Harte

7th grade Social Studies, Vilyon Middle School

***

From: Marcus Watts/Vilyon Middle School/TCPS

To: Sandra Wyatt

Re: Bus Duty

You always wanted to be on Oprah, right? So let's turn this bad situation into a good one. Perhaps you'll go into labor on the bus and one of the kids will deliver the twins. Think of the media coverage. This could be a good thing, Sandra. Maybe you might get offered some free pampers and milk or something. LOL!

Seriously though, poor you. From now on, keep your legs closed if the repercussions will prevent you from performing your assigned duties. For additional questions or comments, please refer to your grade level administration or your employee handbook.

Thanks for putting Vilyon first,

Marcus Watts

6th grade Science, Vilyon Middle School

***

From: Angela Williams/Vilyon Middle School/TCPS

To: Sonya Harte

Re: I know why

She probably dared to question the status quo. It wouldn't surprise me to see her walking out of here with her stuff one of these days. Everything is always perfect as it is. If it isn't, even I know not to openly question it, and I'm dumb as hell.

Angela Williams

8th grade Math, Vilyon Middle School

***

From: Sandra Wyatt/Vilyon Middle School/TCPS

To: Marcus Watts

Re: Bus Duty

Whatever.   How did Peter get on her shit list?   I can't believe she put his name on the list. I can see us because we're always slacking off, but Peter. My goodness, he actually likes these kids. He's not here just because he got laid off from another job either, like some people I know around here.

Sandra Wyatt

6th grade Math, Vilyon Middle School

***

From: Sonya Harte/Vilyon Middle School/TCPS

To: Angela Williams

Re: Hope not

I like Katie Pitts; I think she really cares.   She even helped me with a student who was mouthing off today even though she's not our AP.   She also talked about helping me start that Social Studies Team for all students.   Marsh turned the suggestion down because I said I was going to open it to everyone, not just the gifted students.   If we could have our own elections, I would strike out Marsh for principal and write-in Pitts.

Sonya Harte

7th grade Social Studies, Vilyon Middle School

***

From: Marcus Watts/Vilyon Middle School/TCPS

To: Sandra Wyatt

Re: Bus Duty

Hey, hey with all those snide comments. This is my sixth year. I didn't start out here, but I'm stuck here for life. I'm no longer fit to be in a world where logic, honesty, and respect actually exist. Public education is the only place for me. ☺

Marcus Watts

6th grade Science, Vilyon Middle School

***

From: Angela Williams/Vilyon Middle School/TCPS

To: Sonya Harte

Re: Good administrators

They're honestly so hard to find. Seriously, I hope she stays too. I'm realizing that I can't change this place as a teacher, so I think I'm going to take the Leadership Exam next month. If I can't make a difference as a teacher, I'll do it another way. The next time I see Pitts, I'm going to thank her for making a difference. She has really inspired me.

Angela Williams
8th grade Math, Vilyon Middle School

***

From: Jack Lincoln, Superintendent of Schools/Taylor County

To: Paul Manini, Associated Press News Group

CC: John Smithson—Fox 5 Atlanta, Samantha Scott—Channel 5 Savannah

Re: Today's incident

Per our phone conversations this evening, this information may now be released. Pending a police investigation and official notifications, other details will be released when available.

"This afternoon around 4:10 pm, shots were fired on a sitting Taylor County School bus at Vilyon Middle School. At the time of the shooting, the bus was half filled. No students were injured due to the heroic actions of the Vilyon Middle School Staff. Three staff members were killed: Assistant Principal Katie Pitts, and teachers Peter Pilsher and Sandra Wyatt.

Four suspects are currently being held in police custody.

Vilyon Middle School is the home of the Valiants. Tonight, we salute our valiant staff members and our valiant students who never fail to persevere despite all obstacles and confrontations. As such, parents should rest assured that it will continue to be business as usual at Vilyon Middle School tomorrow. The only exception will be that students and staff will enter the school through a side entry door as opposed to the front door.

Please know that our teachers stand firm in their commitment to your students. They are ready and eager to continue their much-loved tasks of preparing your children for the brightest of futures.

Metal detectors are being installed at all Taylor County Schools as we speak to prevent the possibility of similar situations, and grief counselors will be on hand for the rest of the week to speak to students, parents, and staff as needed. Information regarding the memorial services for our staff members will soon follow.

Thank you for your support and understanding at this time. Our hearts go out to those families who lost loved ones in this tragedy.

Jack Lincoln,

Superintendent of Taylor County Schools

***

Chipped paint, faulty wiring

And broken desks

still linger in many tiny classrooms.

Now they are accompanied

By broken dreams

And shattered lives.

So much has happened

In just the first week of school.

.

www.ingramcontent.com/pod-product-compliance
Lightning Source LLC
Chambersburg PA
CBHW070917180626
46817CB00003B/1099